JF W

Critical acclaim for Nigel Krauth's previous novels:

Matilda, My Darling is a novel of style and originality. Nigel Krauth—remember that name.
Susan Chenery, *Australian Book Review*

Matilda, My Darling is a novel of vigorous power, of mythic proportions and a bloody good yarn.
Gabrielle Lord, *The National Times*

The Bathing Machine Called The Twentieth Century is one of the most refreshingly unpretentious and modestly original new books that I have read.
Helen Elliott, *The Age*

He has produced an entrancing group of characters and, more importantly, an enjoyable story.
Matthew Condon, *The Sun Herald*

ALLEN & UNWIN
FICTION

Nigel Krauth lives with his wife Caron and daughter Alinta on Mount Tamborine in the Gold Coast hinterland and lectures in Literary Studies at the Gold Coast University College. His previous works include *Matilda, My Darling* (co-winner of the *Australian/* Vogel Literary Award) and *The Bathing Machine Called The Twentieth Century* (short-listed for the Victorian Premier's Literary Award and the *Age* Book of the Year Award).

JF Was Here

NIGEL KRAUTH

ALLEN & UNWIN

Sydney   Wellington   London

ACKNOWLEDGEMENTS

The characters and situations in this novel are entirely imaginary and bear no relation to any real person or actual happening.

For the writing of this novel the author was assisted by a fellowship from the Literature Board of the Australia Council and writer's residences at Charles Sturt University—Riverina and Mitchell. For this assistance the author wishes to express his thanks.

First published in 1990
Allen & Unwin Australia Pty Ltd
An Unwin Hyman company
8 Napier Street, North Sydney, NSW 2059, Australia

Allen & Unwin New Zealand Limited
75 Ghuznee Street, Wellington, New Zealand

Unwin Hyman Limited
15–17 Broadwick Street, London W1V 1FP England

National Library of Australia
Cataloguing-in-Publication entry:

Krauth, Nigel, 1949–
JF was here
ISBN 0 04 442283 0
I. Title
A823.3
Text design by Trevor Hood
Series design by Peter Schofield

Set in 10½/12 pt Goudy Old Style, by Graphicraft Typesetters Ltd, Hong Kong
Printed by Australian Print Group, Maryborough, Victoria

In Memoriam
J.W.

a man as sweet as can be
liu liu liu he sings

Warbat tr. Apisai Enos

One stands on the brink of a vast precipice...

*Charles Darwin in the Blue Mountains,
January 17, 1836*

ONE

Getting into the back seat of the taxi, John Freeman saw from the portico of the Hyatt that the world had a fractured look, as if it were painted on shards of glass—ill-fitting, bright, dangerous.

He tried taking deep breaths. They went in and out jaggedly, at odds with the pulse of the city. He tried to refocus his eyes but his perception would not synchronise with the rhythm of pedestrians, traffic, neon signs. There seemed to be too much savage light, as in the effect for which photographers sometimes open their lenses to create a sense of alienation. John looked at the world and knew it was no longer his, felt that it was backing away from him, or speeding past him. A divorce was imminent. He was winding down, and the world was continuing apace.

He would not see the streets of Sydney again, he told himself. As he closed the car door and settled the bulky greatcoat around his narrow body, he heard the thump of his suitcase and his bag of rattling golf sticks being put into the boot by the porter, then the clunk of the boot lid closing. At that moment the driver turned his head around and with horror John realised that the man was black. *Oh, God, Francis. You were right. It's Taxi Number 33.*

'Where to, sir?' The driver's accent was West Indian.

'Medlow Bath. The Hydro Majestic.'

The driver's head twisted around further, almost fully facing his passenger, his forehead puckered in surprise.

'Isn't that up in the Blue Mountains?'

'That's right.'

'But it's a hundred kilometres. I don't usually go that far. Do you have Cabcharge?'

'I've got the money.'

The driver shrugged and turned back to the front. 'I hope you have plenty of money.' He set the car in motion, turning into the traffic.

'I've got it. Don't worry.'

They drove through Kings Cross. John looked at the wet footpaths alive with morning pedestrians, intent, fast moving. All their movement seemed to be away from him. He leant his head against the car window and let the Cross reel by, let the neon flash drunkenly in the heavy winter sky, let the strip clubs and the all-male revue joints fall slowly behind. He closed his eyes for a moment and in his head said goodbye.

Suddenly, in a decision he regretted even as he made it, he said, 'Go up through Darlinghurst. I want to see Oxford Street.'

'As you wish, sir. It's the long way round, sir.' John heard the hint of irony in the driver's voice as he turned obediently left.

They drove down Oxford Street but John could not bear to look. He kept his eyes shut all the way to Whitlam Square and felt the tears edging his eyelids.

Fuck it all, Francis. Fuck the injustice of it. Oh, Jesus, Francis. I am sorry.

John Freeman was going to the Hydro Majestic to die. The suitcase in the boot of the taxi held a few clothes, his music collection, a cassette player, and the dead body of Francis Tapukai. The golf bag held his grandmother, Ina. *Memories have such substance now; the real world seems less convincing.* He felt well enough for the taxi trip. This sudden well-being had in part prompted him to leave the Hyatt. A common and alarming feature of AIDS-related Kaposi's sarcoma was that the sufferer's condition could appear much improved just prior to death.

John had flown to Sydney earlier in the year for the tests. Everyone in the shadowy city streets commented on how warm it was, but he was cold. Fifteen years in the tropics had altered his body's thermometer. The doctors in Sydney all said the same thing: 'Do what you have to, John. Fill up the time. There's no cure yet.' He went back to his hotel and rang Port Moresby. He told the Minister's secretary to post him the compensation payment. He had been Chief Town Planner for the Papua New Guinea Government. They paid him off handsomely: a golden handshake it was called.

He had turned forty on the day the five-figure cheque arrived. Some celebration that was.

At a red light in the city the driver spun his head around. 'Do you want to go out along Parramatta Road, sir? Or across the bridge?'

'It doesn't matter.'

'I only ask because I thought you might prefer the longer way. Touring about are you? Sight-seeing? Have you looked back at the Opera House from Blues Point?'

'I grew up in Sydney. I want to get away from it.'

'Oh, well. The air is much better in the Blue Mountains, I've been told. It's full of eucalyptus given off by the trees. That's why the mountains appear blue when you see them from the coast. I've only been there once myself. I had to take a fare to Katoomba. She said she was chasing after her boyfriend and she thought he was staying up there. I dropped her at Echo Point, but I didn't like leaving her. She was in a real mess. I thought she might jump off one of those cliffs.'

The light changed to green and the driver turned to face the road. He said nothing more, leaving the desperate woman teetering on the cliff edge.

'I'm going to the Hydro because my grandmother went there in 1934.'

'Oh, yes? Visiting your grandmother?'

'She died in 1960.'

The driver did not comment.

'I could just as easily have gone to another hotel in Sydney or Surfers Paradise,' John continued. 'Or Acapulco or Zaire for that matter.'

'Not by taxi, you couldn't.' The driver flashed a chuckling smile into the rear vision mirror.

John looked away. The clutter of cinemas along George Street shivered to fragments and fell behind. *Why did I have to get a driver who was talkative as well as being accusingly black?*

'I've spent four months in the Hyatt with the door locked,' John growled.

'Good Lord. What for?'

'Because if I had come out I might have killed someone.'

The driver gripped the wheel and looked straight ahead.

'And now I know I have killed someone.'

At the Surry Hills Clinic he asked for the facts. He wanted to know everything, for better or worse.

'In your case, John, incredible weight loss (that's already started, of course), severe diarrhoea or major blockages, dehydration perhaps, you might vomit blood. You'll need narcotics, analgesics; morphine most likely. You'll probably feel well too, now and then. Four months is the Australian average. You really should have a friend...'

He mentioned chemotherapy.

'It's very uncomfortable, John. No guarantees, a few months more perhaps is all it offers.'

They weren't really trying to sell it to him. They suggested he have an Ankali Project friend.

'Ankali is an Aboriginal word. It means friend. Just a listener, someone to be there, to help with the anger and the grieving. These people have experience in terminal care, John.'

He said no. He did not want another friend. He left the clinic, extended his booking on a room at the Hyatt, and locked the door. There was a relief in incarceration—he did not have to see his terror reflected in the reactions of others. He played his cassettes and wrote letters to Francis, but received no replies. He only let himself out to visit the clinic.

'Don't you have relatives, John?' the counsellors asked. 'Wouldn't you like contact with the people most important to you? Do you have any unfinished business? Do you really want to do this alone?'

His parents lived in Forster, in the mid-coast retirement belt. He could not face them. They had never adjusted to his being gay, and certainly would not accommodate an HIV positive. He imagined his father wearing surgical gloves and his mother scrubbing the house daily. With them there would be no relief, no forgiveness, no chance of salvation or escape.

'Do what you have to, John. Quite a few withdraw as you are doing, afraid of breaking down and showing it. But there's a difficult experience to come.'

He went back to the Hyatt and played his Tolai music. He had hoped by this not to die alone. In the music Francis came dancing to him, plunged through reef-bright waters, sat darkly in corners. After four months the cassette tapes were thin and scratchy. He received at last a letter from Port Moresby. It wasn't written by Francis. It said that Francis was dead.

Throughout the deep despair, the suicidal self-hatred, the whole shattering breakdown, the morphine killed the physical pain. But the music... *Francis' music*. He kept playing the music. He had killed Francis.

Waking this morning feeling strange, feeling oddly better in fact, it had occurred to him that he had another friend: his grandmother, Ina. Desperately he thought it out again: she was the only member of his family, perhaps the only person in the world, who would have understood in any way. She too had been an outcast, a dupe of history, a victim and a killer. She lived for twenty-five years with her dark burden and with the terror of her guilt. At the thought of Ina, it seemed to John that a window opened.

He gathered his things, locked his suitcase, and had called for the Hyatt porter.

One night in Port Moresby, driving home from a party at the Travelodge and trying to avoid the drunken traffic on Sir Hubert Murray Drive, John heard Francis tell a story. It was a Papua New Guinean legend: not a legend from the village but from the town. Slumped down in the passenger seat beside John, Francis recounted it in loping, drunken syllables, peeling it from the wealth of stories he carried in his head, knowing it was a good enough item to repay John for the evening drinks, for all the evening activities yet to come.

A taxi roared past them where the highway turned up from Ela Beach. The accelerating car disappeared into the darkness ahead, leaving no trace. Its tail lights weren't working.

'Ah, *poro*. Don't ever get into Taxi Number 33,' Francis drawled, his voice full of portent.

'Why's that, mate?'

'Because it's a ghost taxi, *poro*. It only turns up late at night. Suppose you are walking along a dark road, just hoping a taxi will come along. And suddenly it does. It comes up behind you. It stops and the door opens by itself. You get into the back seat and the rattling door closes. Before you can even say where you want to go the taxi starts off. It picks up speed. Then at last the driver turns around towards you. His head turns around, and keeps on turning, around and around and around. Or perhaps his head turns around and he has a bleeding, fly-ridden skull's face. *Aiyee*. You want to jump out of the speeding car but you can't. There are no handles on the door. You must keep on going. And you know where you are going, *poro*?'

'No idea.'

'To hell.'

Francis broke into high-pitched laughter, and John joined in.

'I'll remember that, mate. Taxi Number 33.'

'To hell direct, *poro*. No stops.'

John watched the wintry parklands of the university warp across the glass of the taxi window. Wanting to think about Ina, he believed he glimpsed a figure, far-off through the oak trees by an ornamental lake, swinging a golf club, hitting practice balls on a cold sweep of lawn.

Is it Ina?

No, that wasn't Ina. How could she be out there? If anyone was truly his fellow passenger in Taxi Number 33, it was her.

TWO

At the wharf Ina could have enquired about the departure time of the daily service on the Western Line through Medlow Bath, but she did not bother. She did not care whether she had spare time or not. Sydney did not interest her. She had not even gone up on deck when the steamer passed under the new Harbour Bridge. The burden of her rage was too great. She left the steamer and caught a taxi from the Sussex Street wharf up to Central Station. She walked angrily into the station and found the refreshment room. She sat at a table, impolitely ordered a pot of tea and considered the horror of cities: traffic and trouble, concrete and crime. Civilised man's progress! It appalled her now. For several hours she sat in the refreshment room, going through pots of tea. All the while, her bag of golf clubs leant against the table's edge; she did not trust it to the porters in the baggage room.

On the train she was overcome with scorn at the ugliness of humanity. The pallid-skinned passengers sickened her. 'Where do they crawl from,' she asked herself, 'the people on trains?' She wished she had hired a car. There was no relief outside the smudged window. The narrow backyards of Redfern, having succumbed to black locomotive smoke, flickered by like doomed frames in an old movie.

After the train trip Ina stood on the platform at Medlow Bath station with her legs apart and her golf bag slung over her right shoulder. Her thought was: 'It's bloody cold and I shall need a fur coat.' She gave the porter from the Hydro the same look she had developed for Papuan boys over the past sixteen years. It was a look which said simply: 'Watch out.' The porter did not appreciate it.

'Is it always this cold?' she demanded.

'Today's mild, ma'am,' the porter informed her. 'Middle of winter's much worse, ma'am.'

She looked at the fallen leaves and the late-blooming *Lonicera* in tubs on the platform. The flowers were smutty. 'I won't like it here either,' she said, setting off towards the overhead stairs.

The porter followed. Noting the stickers on her luggage, he said, 'Medlow is nothing like the tropics, ma'am.'

And she thought, 'Thank God.'

The hotel was right across the road from the station. She allowed the porter to lead her through the gates and along the gravel drive where a black car stood with its motor idling, blowing blue smoke. There were bushes of *Lavandula spica* beside the drive and beyond them to her left she saw players on the croquet green. She gave them a dark look as she kept walking. 'Croquet is nothing like golf,' she thought bitterly. 'Nothing like life. No bunkers, no hazards.'

'Damn you all,' she said out loud to the doorman's welcoming smile.

Remembering Ina was a distraction from remembering Francis, but John needed more than that. His parents had brought him up believing there was only guilt and shame to be found in tracing his blood back through Ina; but that guilt and shame seemed as nothing now to the utter helpless despair, to the hatred of death and life both, in tracing his blood forward to Francis.

Ina had seen a man die in Moresby and had shut the guilt inside her until one shattering day, twenty-five years later, when she let it all back out again. She came and stood at the edge of the Hydro's swimming pool where Johnno was splashing with other twelve-year-old boys, and called him out of the water. He dragged himself up onto the pool's crazy-paved surround, hearing her say, 'Follow me'. He followed her to her room and she locked the door and sat him dripping wet on the bed. Then she settled herself into the room's only chair. *I have something to tell you, Johnno.*

And while Ina's end was to be his end, it seemed, so too had it been his beginning. He was Ina's child much more than he was his parents'. She had on that day taught him the monstrousness of the world and of the people in it. Through her he had seen how dignity, justice, hope, were idiotic lies, how madness was the norm, how independence was impossible yet you saved yourself or were not saved at all. In short, she had opened his eyes, she had set him on his path.

Ina's blood coursed madly in his veins. It made him what he was, he realised. He needed to acknowledge it.

Inside the Hydro Ina did not give herself to the stunning view. Once, in the past, she would have looked out the large windows of the lounge and gone right over the sheer drop plummetting a thousand feet into that marvellous gulf. But there was thin response from her senses now: a meanness born of bitterness and compelling hatred. There was nothing to match the gulf inside her.

She had been a sensualist in spite of conventions, even in spite of government ordinances. In surviving she had let her senses make decisions for her. Others had seen it as indulgent and worse, she realised now. Until the hanging she had never thought herself vulnerable or wrong, just ill-fitting, as if Fate selected the wrong club each time it played a stroke towards her destiny.

Standing at the window overlooking the deep valley, she saw the snow on the far peaks beyond Oberon, and thought to herself, 'Thank God, I'm away from the Equator.'

THREE

They took the Western Freeway. John tried to ignore the driver's 'Voice of the Guidebook' commentary, pitched in an alien accent. West Indian convicts transported to Australia. Black Caesar, the first bushranger. Billie Blue, the Negro ferryman, replaced ultimately by the Harbour Bridge. Viv Richards and the Brisbane Tied Test. His own application for citizenship. John hardly recognised the country being spoken of. He rested his head against the upholstery of the taxi, knowing he did not have the guts or the right to beg the driver to shut up. He saw the blue gleam on the skin of the driver's neck, just above the collar where the tight, pubic-like curls of hair started, and tried yet again not to think about poor dead Francis in the suitcase in the boot.

At the end of the Western Freeway, where the highway turned upwards through the foothills of the mountains, John rolled the window down a little, hoping to hear the bellbirds. He remembered their call from his childhood trips. Twice a year his parents would drive to the Hydro for holidays and he would hear the pure, distilled sound of the birds calling in the dense eucalypt forests beside the winding road. But the sound was elusive as salvation itself, and he received through the open window only the rush of cold mountain air and the sight of naked earth in cuttings topped with thinning eucalypts falling quickly behind.

The taxi halted in the drive of the hotel. The driver pressed a switch and John heard the boot lid spring open. Fumbling in his

wallet, John pulled out the money.
It was far too much, and yet nothin
'Thank you. Please keep the chang
The driver turned his head around an
He clambered out quickly to remove Jc
boot.

There followed, at the back of the car, a   ine
bags. John did not want the black man to ca   ...side the
hotel. He found the strength to be adamant. ...ter lifting the
bags from the boot the driver put them down on the gravel and
retreated. 'As you wish, sir,' he smiled, and got back into the
car.

The taxi left. John Freeman stood in the drive of the hotel
with the strap of the golf bag over his left shoulder and the
handle of the suitcase in his right hand. He curled his back
against the strain of lifting. The suitcase did not budge. Above
him the domed roofs and pillared balconies of the Hydro Majestic teetered.

He took the weight and lifted.

John leant against the reception desk, panting. After two hours
in the taxi, carrying his suitcase along with the golf bag had
been stupid. He let the breath travel in and out, raspingly. He
concentrated his attention on his bowels where the reaction
would come, if it came. Behind the desk the reception clerk
straightened the heart-shaped stud in his left ear and gave John
an appraising look.

'I made a booking. John Freeman.'

The clerk ran the tip of his ball-point down the open page.
'Oh, yes.' He looked up. There was an expression of oblique
challenge on his face. 'A single?'

John outgazed him, catching his breath.

'Yes.' *Has he guessed? The bitch.*

The clerk looked down at the book again. 'Room 220.' He
took the key from the board behind him and held it out across
the desk. John made him put it into his hand. Their fingers
touched, and the clerk withdrew his. 'In the New Wing,' the
clerk said. 'Just up the stairs.'

..ated. More stairs. And he was not sure that he
co be in the *New* Wing.

want a room where I can feel something of the hotel's
istory.'

The clerk's hand went to the stud in his ear again. 'All our
rooms have "Nostalgic charm", sir.' He closed his eyes in a long
blink.

John put the key into his pocket. 'I'll need someone to carry
my luggage up.'

FOUR

Before going up to his room John crossed the lounge and put his fingers gingerly to the pane of one of the huge windows. The view was breath-taking, but he had little breath to spare. From the activity around him it was obvious that the Hydro Majestic was in the middle of another face-lift. The lounge was being extended further out over the gorge, more large windows were being put in to capture more of the view. For the builders it was dangerous work. The men clinging to scaffolding on the outside of the building were buffeted by wind which swept up the cliffs from the valley floor. They hammered and drilled while their hair was torn sideways. Yet they seemed unperturbed, even jovial. From their wild element they ogled John through the window. They were getting good danger money, he supposed.

He turned away to look back across the lounge. In the corridors leading from the lobby the workmen seemed to out-number the guests. They pushed barrows on chipboard catwalks laid down to protect the carpets; they hammered at stud-walls. John hoped their clatter would cease in the evenings.

On the visits his family had made in the 'fifties Johnno had explored the Hydro in the company of other holidaying kids, and he had grown to expect that Ina's room would be some-where different each visit. *I don't like that room any more, Johnno. I've moved to this one now.* Sometimes she overlooked the gorge, sometimes the pool and the lavender gardens. During the intervening decades, he realised now, the great sprawl of the hotel had not shrunk an inch, as tended to happen to most scales and distances remembered from childhood. The Hydro Majestic was still a monstrosity.

'Still the longest building in the southern hemisphere,' a helpful worker informed him from behind a wheelbarrow. 'In the *Guinness Book of Records*, mate. You'll need a street directory to find your way about.'

For each changed era during three-quarters of a century the Hydro had undergone a face-lift: Art Nouveau, Art Deco, Frank Lloyd Wright, suburban kitsch. Each era was built over, covered in, boxed around, like Kurt Schwitters' *mertzbau*, until there were walls behind walls behind walls with the dust of history in dark cavities between. But some things never changed: the plummeting, hypnotising view; the frightening fascination of the cliff edge; the wind carving tirelessly at the sandstone beneath the hotel's foundations.

John noticed that his luggage had gone from in front of the reception desk. He checked the room number on his key-tag, then headed for the stairs in the corner of the lounge where a sign said: 'New Wing'. He tackled the stairs uncertainly. Two flights up he was panting again. He hauled himself the last few steps by clinging to the gilded handrail.

He found Room 220. It was at the top of the stairs, set aside at the end of its own short corridor. From his sense of the building he reckoned the room to be one of the highest on the valley side. He fumbled with his key in the lock, then opened the door onto 1947. A starkness of original post-war furniture and fittings greeted him. Entirely depressing. Nostalgic charm? He had been born in 1947. He gauged the New Wing to be almost as old as he was. He crossed to the draughty window and closed the curtains against the mad plunge of the view.

His suitcase had been left on the luggage stand just inside the door. He turned to it, lowered his thumbs to the locks, and froze. He recalled his horror when as a child he had first seen a ventriloquist's dummy pushed into its suitcase at the end of a performance. The dummy had kept on screaming in a muffled, accusatory way as the ventriloquist carried the suitcase from the stage.

John did not open the suitcase. He lay down on the bed to rest.

FIVE

He rang reception and ordered another taxi.

It was madness, he knew. He should have rested to conserve his strength. He felt odd, tired and vulnerable. Everything in the room seemed tilted slightly. But he was driven by a nervous excitement. Thoughts of Ina whirred inside him.

This is the truth, Johnno. And don't you ever let anyone tell you otherwise.

He remembered how she sat with her back to the lace-curtained window which overlooked the gorge. She had seemed unconcerned about the water dripping off his body onto the chenille quilt.

Your parents may tell tales about me, but they don't know what happened. They have only read the newspapers, like everyone else.

He went slowly down the stairs to the lounge. There was a hollowness behind his eyes but he felt remarkably strong. Perhaps it wasn't a mistake to use the energy while he had it.

It all began in Cowra, Johnno, with those perverted aunts of mine peering at me through the cracks in the outhouse wall.

He stood in the warm lobby and looked out at the dusk hanging in the bare branches of trees in the garden. When the taxi came up the drive he stepped from the warmth, drawing the hug of the greatcoat around his body.

I never found a husband, Johnno. Not a real one. Men don't know how to be husbands.

In the taxi his excitement grew. He had to keep reminding himself that he wasn't actually going to meet Ina, and that he should not expect too much of the places where her memory might still have currency. But he was gripped by an urgency to find her name.

The world works by betrayals, Johnno. Do you know what I mean by that?

The taxi dropped him at the Blackheath Golf Club. It was not far from the hotel: only $6.40 showed on the meter. A bitter wind blew up from the grey fairways but it did not diminish the excitement swelling in him. As he strained against the heavy door to the clubhouse he wondered what a celebratory glass of wine would do to him now.

I went to Papua because I was in love with a man called Andrew Prideaux. Your mother probably hasn't mentioned him, Johnno, but what is the point of you not knowing?

In the club lounge the first things John saw were the two champions boards. High gloss timber, gold lettering. He looked at the smaller one, knowing it would be the associates' roll. And because he knew the dates—1935 to 1939—his eye landed on her name almost immediately. Five years running she had been the club's women's champion. He stood transfixed by the golden column of the name's repetition:

> INA L. STOCKS
> INA L. STOCKS
> INA L. STOCKS
> INA L. STOCKS
> INA L. STOCKS

. . . After all those invisible footprints around the course, she had left this golden spoor descending on highly polished wood. Lest the present club members forget.

The other man's name was Vaimuru, Johnno. But they called him Stephen V. in the papers. He was hanged by the neck. They said he and I did something stupid together. I will never get over it. I saw the rope go under his chin and I watched as his tongue shot out. I will curse the world for it forever, and I will curse myself.

There was no triumph for him in seeing his grandmother's name enshrined. He stood and waited for some magic to occur but in the fluorescent glare of the clubhouse lighting nothing happened. No ghost appeared, conjured by his possession of her name.

He had expected something salutory. He had hoped for a vital link with her, but he thought instead of another. Her name, stepped in gold down the board towards him, made him think of the Golden Staircase, and of Francis Tapukai. Of the lewdness and delight of coupling and joking on the Kokoda Trail. Of their well-worn, lovingly worn jokes about the Cock-odour Trail. Ha. Such word play. Such pathetic, childish, desperately happy love play. The things they did!

The mad idea of risking a celebratory drink at the bar, barely conceived, had fled. He turned back to the red phone at the lounge door and called for another taxi.

On a gallows far down a hill in his mind a figure was hanging. He zoomed towards it unsuccessfully, losing direction, coming up against a backdrop of sharply glinting sea in grainy, over-exposed light.

SIX

John woke late on his first morning at the Hydro. He sat up in bed and checked his watch. It was after nine. He rummaged in the shaving-kit which he had put beside the bed. The pills were there. He closed his eyes as he swallowed them. Pills for appetite, pills for diarrhoea, pills for pain. They reminded him of his despair. He didn't want to be reminded of that. But they were better than the injections. He had stopped giving himself the injections. He had morphine he could take from a spoon now. But he avoided that too, if he could. It made him dislocated, nauseous. He lay back on the pillow with his hand at his throat, aware of the trail left by the dry pills, feeling also the area where the elongated lumps of his lymph glands had been. If only they would swell and go knotty again, to show that his system was fighting. Even a flabbiness there—that over-cooked macaroni feel—would be encouraging; at least that might indicate a rearguard action. But the glands were shrivelled away to nothing. Not the hint of a lump. Like the neck of a perfectly healthy person.

He cleared his throat and thought about breakfast but he had no appetite. The ghost of last night's exhaustion still clung to him: a wobbly feeling behind the eyes. He looked around the room at the lacquered furniture and the wallpaper peeling near the cornice above the door. Then he noticed the corner of a newspaper poking under the door. He got up and fetched it and took it back to bed with him.

That worldwide ritual, that keenness to know the state of life on the planet: the opening of the paper each day. It had always fascinated him. The familiar size of the pages, the predictable layout. No matter what country, what language: the horror story on the front, the girl on page three (non-Muslim countries), world news page five, sport at the back. Yet reading the paper was a new experience every morning, the crossing of a frontier forever unknown, like playing again a golf course one has played and played. Always the same, always different.

He could not remember a time when he didn't read the morning newspaper. As a boy he used to get it sheet by sheet at the breakfast table, after his father had finished with each page. He had liked the sport best then, the back page, especially the golf and the boxing: Arnold Palmer, Gary Player, Floyd Paterson, 'Sugar' Ray...The front page had been interesting only when a celebrated murder had occurred. Then he would pore over the details, especially if a photograph was printed with crosses or dotted lines superimposed.

X—VICTIM STABBED HERE————
X—BODY FOUND HERE————
X—MURDER WEAPON DISCOVERED HERE.

Against the static, innocuous black and white background of some dull suburban street or anonymous stretch of coastline he imagined torrid realities—cruel, blood-spattered dramas whose vividness he found all the more alarming for being stepped out in plain white crosses and dashes.

One case he particularly recalled occurred when he was in first year at high school. The Graeme Thorne Kidnap Case. The photograph on the front page of the *Sydney Morning Herald* showed the block of flats at Bondi where the Thorne family lived. A dotted line went around the corner and down the street to the local cake shop and a cross:

X—BOY LAST SEEN HERE.

Graeme Thorne had set off for school in the morning, had purchased his daily cupcake treat, then disappeared. His father had just won the £100 000 Opera House Lottery. The ransom demand from the kidnapper was for £25 000.

Before going to school each morning Johnno had devoured the facts in the case along with his Weet-Bix and milk and sugar. Suddenly the story had lifted off the pages of the newspaper and entered his own life. On the third day Graeme Thorne's schoolbag was found behind the monument on the Wakehurst Parkway just a few streets away from Johnno's house in Seaforth Crescent. That afternoon, after school, he rode to the monument on his bicycle. He expected a crowd of people, police, detectives, but there was only the discoloured sandstone with its metal plaque and some evidence of trampling in the bush close behind it. The cars on the Parkway rushed by regardless.

Then came the stunner. Several weeks later the front page showed a photograph of a shelf of rock on a vacant block of land. A big cross indicated:

X—BODY FOUND HERE.

Dead and wrapped in a travelling rug, Graeme Thorne had been discovered by kids playing in one of the streets Johnno rode along to school each day. That morning he stopped off at the vacant block, laid his bike down in the liver-coloured pebbles beside the unkerbed road, and walked up to the rock ledge. The houses on either side presented curtained windows, blank fences. He looked into the shallow recess under the rock shelf and imagined the rolled blanket, the form within it, the dead boy's face. And even though events, history, the news, had been and gone and whisked Graeme Thorne's body away, Johnno felt that history emerge from its anonymity and claim him personally, because the only face he could visualise for the boy was his own.

The case unfolded further in the morning papers. Investigations, clues, rewards for information, forensic evidence. Months later, when the kidnapper, Stephen Bradley, was arrested in Ceylon, and the house he had rented in nearby Clontarf appeared in pictures in the paper, Johnno convinced his father to drive him there so that he could look down the driveway at the infamous pink double-garage door. Behind that door Graeme Thorne had been locked in the boot of Bradley's car for several days, bound and gagged, and had died when the kidnapper had been surprised by his unwitting family, causing him to crash the lid of the boot hurriedly down on Graeme's raised head. PWANG!

That was 1960. After that, Johnno thought often of Graeme Thorne in the boot of his captor's car—slung in there along with a bag of golf clubs—living in the black darkness. Perhaps it was the detail of the golf clubs that caused Johnno to identify with Graeme Thorne just a little too much? Golf was part of Johnno's family heritage. Ina had been a champion—at least that's how the family put it when they spoke about her at all. His father played too. There was always a set of clubs and a folded buggy in the boot of the family car. But his father never taught him to play, never took him to caddy even, because his mother forbad it.

'One golf champion in the family is bad enough,' she would say, turning away in the manner she always used when the subject of Ina was brought up.

'Why, Mum?' Johnno would ask.

'I just don't like golf.'

Such talk angered his father. 'Have a bit of consideration, son.'

Johnno judged for himself that, yes, you could live in the darkness of a car boot for a while, lying quietly, the bones aching, remembering the sunlight, thinking of your family and Weet-Bix and the morning papers, with your head against the spare tyre and the golf bag at your back, the smell of leather and wood and rubber in your nostrils. But Graeme Thorne had made the mistake of lifting his head when his frightened kidnapper came to check that he was all right. He shouldn't have lifted his head.

That was 1960. In the same year the Freemans drove across the mountains from Sydney to Bloomfield for Ina's funeral. In the middle of the Graeme Thorne Kidnap Case (so it seemed to Johnno) his grandmother had gone mad (as his father put it) and died. At the Bloomfield crematorium, while the golfing fraternity stood around with long faces, and his mother stood stonily tearless, Johnno watched the gristly brown smoke (thick and curling like pubic hair, he thought) rise from the crematorium chimney.

21

'That's her,' he said out loud, pointing at the smoke.

'For God's sake, Johnno,' his mother had forced between clenched teeth. But even then she did not cry.

On the way back over the mountains his father booked a night at the Hydro Majestic. Partly out of nostalgia, partly to wind up Ina's affairs at the hotel. The next morning, while his parents took a walk down one of the Hydro's bush tracks, Johnno masturbated fretfully in the hotel room and was shocked again by the pearl which oozed like a tear at the end of his member.

In the family Ina was called Ina—never Mum or Gran— partly because she had abrogated her responsibilities as mother and grandmother, and the family never forgave her; partly because of her infamy; but mostly because that was the way she wanted it. Stories about Ina's life were told with reticence by her daughter Louise, Johnno's mother. And she never mentioned the several stains that Ina had left on the family history...the husbands she deserted, the children she abandoned, the business of the hanging in New Guinea. Certainly, after Ina was arrested in her sixty-fifth year on the cliff top at Medlow Bath—poised, legs apart, just beginning a downswing with her seven-iron—and whisked off to Bloomfield Mental Asylum, the subject of Ina was as good as banned in the Freeman house.

And the more the Freemans tried to keep Ina in the dark, the more deeply young Johnno buried within himself and kept sacred what he knew of her. But the story of her life which Ina had told him remained diffuse as an unassembled jig-saw puzzle. Its constituent pieces disturbed him too greatly: he never examined them. He never tried to put them together to see the full picture.

John closed the newspaper. He went to the bathroom and sat with his head in his hands for a long time. His bowels griped as if they had knots in them.

SEVEN

Ina was born in 1895—a fact which came to light only after her death when her birth certificate was discovered; she always lied about her age. She grew up in Cowra, reared by two Seventh Day Adventist aunts who prohibited the reading of books in their house. Throughout her childhood Ina had to smuggle reading matter strapped to her stomach from the council library to her room and then down the backyard path to the outhouse. There, in the fetid warmth rising around the pan she read by the cracks of light coming between the weatherboards. Her aunts' suspicions were raised by the length of time she spent in the dimness of the outhouse. At times they came to peek in on her through the cracks. *'What are you doing in there? Are you being wicked?'* *That's what they would say to me, Johnno.* But she managed the deception without ever being caught.

This prohibited reading aroused in her a passion for print and publishing. Out of spite for her aunts and their narrow religion she was determined to become a journalist. At the age of fifteen, armed with an excellent report from her school head-mistress, she took a job as tea-girl with the town newspaper, the Cowra *Clarion.* For a year she pushed the tea-trolley and answered the telephone. She developed a special telephonist's voice—'Hellooo, Cowra Cla-ri-on'—which she never used at her aunts' house. And she found a spot down by the bridge where she applied and removed her make-up on the walk to and from work. At sixteen (but saying she was twenty-one) she applied successfully for a reporter's position on the *Wagga Advertiser.* Her aunts went with her to the railway station. A constant babble of precautions and prohibitions issued from their lips. She listened to none of it. In her mind the door of the outhouse was opening and the sun was streaming in. She boarded the train in a daze of wonder. On the platform her aunts waved hesitantly, but she forgot to look back at them. She watched out the window the entire way to Wagga. To her the world seemed brilliant and wide.

EIGHT

Suddenly John felt hopeful. For a moment, and in spite of the pain in his gut and the reddened water in the bowl when he looked down, he was experiencing a feeling of being at one with himself, as if a hand had adjusted a lens and brought his perception of self into brief focus—unblurred him, as it were. Surrounded by the unpromising 'forties plumbing he had a fleeting sense of ascendancy, a flashback to himself standing with Francis on a high ridge in New Guinea, with Francis throwing his head back and laughing, his mouth full of teeth without a single filling.

John still did not dare to open the suitcase. He picked up the clothes he had thrown on the floor the night before and dressed in them again. He felt motivated to move, to ignore his enervated body. The cold weather, made obvious by the inefficiency of the steam heating, demanded that he dress warmly. He remembered his clothes abandoned in the wardrobe in the Sydney Hyatt. Some nice find for the cleaning staff, he imagined. All those new winter clothes—the leather, the wool— too large for him already. But he had worn the woollen great-coat, there was no point in leaving that behind. It seemed he now felt the cold more sharply, more stressfully, just as he had felt the heat more severely in Port Moresby before he left. That was the way it was. His body was less well defended, more acutely sensitive. Perhaps his mind was too? He looked at the suitcase and in his vision it seemed to swell. *What it contains is bloating still.* Village music, hot nights. He turned away from it.

As he pulled on his clothes he remembered an old bow

tie—the big red polka-dotted bow tie he had always worn at conferences. Ha! Those town planners' conferences where he had given papers. He had made quite a reputation for himself, an international reputation, not so much for the content of his addresses, but for the flair of his delivery. Attached to the bow tie was a wire which ran under his collar to a little battery and switch in his pants pocket. At a pressure on the switch the bow tie blurred into a whirring propeller. It had always caused a stir and, as he remembered, provided a necessary bright spot of comedy. Town planners were generally dull types, he had thought. Their conferences were a torment to anyone the least bit lively. He considered himself one of the first in the southern hemisphere to recognise that cities should be planned for fun as well as serious function. With the bow tie spinning at his throat, he had attacked his peers' rigid notions of the city as super-machine. That was more than a decade ago: the 'hard-edge, minimalist' era. Planning was more relaxed now, ideas of the city more organic and human-oriented. Cities laughed now, cracked jokes at their own expense.

He tried to remove the bow tie from his mind. He had been a bit of a showman, he supposed. He had liked laughter and silliness. He knew he had played the fool on occasion to conceal concern or a sense of inferiority, or sometimes terror.

And perhaps this is all showmanship now, he thought, imagining himself unmanageably ill in the hotel bed, imagining the trouble his body would give the management.

In his mind the bow tie whirred again.

Stuff them.

Already wearing his heavy coat John went down to the lounge. He enquired at the desk about a booklet on the history of the Hydro.

'There isn't one yet,' said the girl behind the desk, fiddling with the ring on her left hand. 'There's a reproduction of an old poster. And the postcards.'

She showed him copies. He bought sets of them, putting them on his bill.

'Can you tell me about the wing I am in—the New Wing? It

was built around '46, '47, wasn't it?' The girl's face went blank. 'My grandmother was a long-term resident here,' he continued. 'From '34 to '60. Except for the war, of course. Is there some sort of register of famous guests? She was a well-known golfer and journalist.'

The girl blinked several times rapidly. So much information coming at her out of the void!

'I suppose you could talk to Mrs West. She is one of the owners.'

This was said in a vaguely annoyed way, as if his enquiry—as if the past itself—were something equal in importance to a lost sock or a complaint about the absence of a page in a Gideon's Bible.

'I could make an appointment for you,' she added, remembering courtesy to guests.

'I'd like that,' John said, and the girl looked around for a piece of paper on which to write a note.

John spent the rest of the morning wandering, getting lost, re-finding his way, in the corridors of the hotel building. He ignored signs which said: 'Staff Only Permitted Beyond This Point'. He walked along corridor after silent corridor where dim lights burned but all the doors were locked. Plainly, most of the hotel's rooms were unused. He turned back on stairways that led up or down to blank walls and he startled at the sound of creaking doors in dark abandoned passageways where no doors were obvious. He recognised no door or hallway as ever having been specifically Ina's; they were all vaguely familiar, yet unfamiliar too. There were no signs, no dotted lines, no fingers in gold leaf pointing: THIS WAY TO INA.

Wherever he went there was darkness, dimly lit. Between him and the grand plummetting views of the valley there were locked doors and empty rooms. He travelled solely in the bowels of the building, never getting near its skin, it seemed. He noticed great patches of carpet where the pile was mossed with damp or bared by rats' chewing. He negotiated dark landings that swayed under his feet. He was thumped by suddenly swinging doors which closed on him in vestibules where his weight made the thresholds sink. In the course of his study as a planner he had been in many buildings due for demolition, but never in one which had seemed to him so hideously cancerous yet still hauntingly alive. Even in the farthest wings the lamps continued to flicker, but in a tired way, suggesting they should have been turned off decades ago. And wherever he put his hand on the endless central heating pipes he felt the warmth still sighing in them, like a ghostly heat left over from some great gone decade. Feeling claustrophobic, he said out loud as if the building itself might reply, 'Which of these rooms did Ina stay in? Which was her corridor?' He couldn't remember.

A workman with a black face appeared suddenly around a corner and surprised him where he stood with his hand on a pipe.

'Most of the place is condemned, mate,' the workman said. 'Foundations are buggered.' The black face smiled as it went by into the gloom.

NINE

At the Wagga *Advertiser* Ina was put on the sport and social columns. On the first day the editor, Walter Lumsden, a peppery man in his forties, yelled at her across his desk as his blue pencil slashed through her work.

'Don't tell me you don't play a sport, girl!' As if such a thing were tantamount to treason. 'Haven't you learnt the rules of any game?'

She looked back, wide-eyed with fear. 'I have played tennis, sir. But not bothered with the rules.'

'Not bothered?' Lumsden was flabbergasted. 'Go to the library then. Read up on rules.'

He dismissed her with a backhand wave.

On her third day at the paper Lumsden called her in again. He turned his freckled face up at her from his desk. Pointedly he crushed her copy between his hands.

'It's called a cricket bat, my dear,' he bellowed, 'not a paddle.'

She wondered if she were about to get fired.

'And in your story on the golf tournament you've listed the place-getters in reverse order. It's the *lowest* score wins in golf!'

He stood up and hurled the ball which her copy had become towards the wastepaper basket in the corner.

'Get your coat,' he growled. 'You can carry the bag.'

She thought maybe 'carry the bag' meant the same as 'get the sack'.

'Well, get a move on, girl,' Lumsden said from the door. 'You have to start somewhere. It might as well be with me.'

That was a Wednesday afternoon and Walter Lumsden always played a round of golf at the nine-hole Wagga course on Wednesday afternoons to steady his nerves.

They drove to the course in his Model T Ford. It was her first ride in a car. It was also the first time she walked on fairways, raked bunkers, trod gingerly on greens, and it was a baptism of fire.

'This is called "Addressing the ball",' Lumsden said at the first tee. He had a funny way of flapping his elbows and giving his right leg a rubbery shake as he did this, but even Ina in her ignorance could see that these were eccentricities specific to his game and not part of the general rules.

'I see,' she said helpfully.

'And this is the backswing.' He held the head of the club poised in the air for an imperious moment then brought it down fast. PWANG! The ball squirted off to the right.

'That's a slice. Okay?' he snarled, retrieving his tee.

Peering ahead from the rough at the dog-leg she watched his ball glide high then plummet rapidly. It seemed to go into a hole and stay there, not bouncing at all. Was that a hole in one? she wondered. Luckily, she did not dare to say it out loud.

'It's in the bloody bunker,' Lumsden bellowed.

When the ball was finally in the hole she thought he would be pleased. But he wasn't. On the track towards the second tee he pointed with his gloved finger at the space on the score card where she should write the numeral '6'.

'It's called a flamin' double bogey. Have you got that?' he raged.

She followed the freckles on his face. They danced more and more convulsively as the round progressed. In the small clubhouse after the ball had dropped nine merciful times, he found her a lemonade and himself a whisky (from his marked bottle on the shelf) and they settled back in the frayed chairs among the handmowers and the flags and fertiliser. In a gravelly-wistful voice, not his usual gravelly-angry voice, he said:

'There's no sport like it. Fresh air. Natural surroundings. No opponents. No violence. Just yourself and your ego labouring away.'

She sipped her lemonade and took mental notes.

'It's the simplest game, the most obvious game. A monkey with a stick can play it. And there are very few rules. It must be the game with the least number of rules. That ought to suit you, Ina.'

He talked and drank until the sunset bathed the pale fairways in a pink light. A pink light which entered the clubhouse windows and grew as fierce as did the flush on Lumsden's face.

'Golf's a progress, Ina. A fashion parade, if you like. A pastoral. A dance. A journey. An expedition. A hunt. A quest. A passion. A love affair. A nightmare. A battlefield. An addiction.'

She remembered it all.

'But, Ina dear, I'll let you into a secret. The real *blessing* of golf is this...' He drained his whisky glass yet again. 'Golf's a glimpse of Elysium.'

Out of her first week's pay she put on lay-by at the Wagga Cash Store a beginner's set of hickory-shafted clubs.

Her earliest assignments for the social column were less traumatic. A school fete and a clergyman's retirement were handled with ease. The first civic function she attended was the supper which followed the stepping down of the old mayor, Alderman Stocks, and the investiture of his replacement, Alderman Grieves. She hovered just inside the city hall, feeling nervous and exposed under an electric light. She was unfamiliar with the Who's Who of Wagga Wagga society. She had read up on the more prominent names, but could not put faces to them. The only person she knew in the crowd was Walter Lumsden. Every time his stare turned her way she pretended to be in chatty conversation with the person nearest her. One of the guests to whom she directed a staged nod and a silently mouthed greeting took her up in actual conversation. She could not have made a better choice of informant: Tom Stocks was the retiring mayor's son.

'That's Dad. Over there,' Tom said. 'Mum's with him. That's Bob Grieves beside her. And his wife...'

Tom gave her a comprehensive commentary on all the guests

(both present and significantly absent), their achievements (both printable and unprintable), and the order in which they should be mentioned in the column. She took surreptitious notes on a little pad clasped in the palm of her hand, but it was done with difficulty for Tom had fetched her a dainty biscuit and a glass of sherry which she juggled, at the same time trying to follow his gaze as it subtly pinpointed individuals around the hall.

'That's Nugent the butcher. "Bully" Nugent we call him. He only takes female carcasses. Reckons the meat's more tender. And that's Mrs Greenwood. Always got a mosquito on the end of her nose. You look.'

She laughed. She liked Tom's wickedness. *I found him attractive, Johnno, because I knew my aunts would disapprove. But I'm talking about nice wickedness, you understand. Liveliness, you could call it.*

When supper was announced they sat together at one of the long tables. She learnt that he (at only twenty-four years of age) had just taken over from his father as head of the family business. The old man was retiring from work to coincide with his retirement from politics. Yes, Tom Stocks was now managing director of the Wagga Cash Store—the very same where her golf clubs were on lay-by. Tom promised her personal service each time she came in to make a payment.

After the closing speeches Walter Lumsden swooped by. 'How's it going, Little Tom?'

Tom winced at the sobriquet. Against Lumsden's amused glare he said, 'Just taking care of the *Advertiser's* new acquisition, Mr Lumsden.'

The freckles flared on Lumsden's face. 'Not putting your fingers on the merchandise, I hope.'

'I wouldn't think of it, sir,' Tom said quickly.

'Well, I'm taking her off display now,' Lumsden said. He had his hands on the back of her chair, ready to help her away from the table. His eyes were bloodshot with the sherry. 'Journalist's first rule. Never stay to the end of anything.'

Tom stood and offered her his hand. 'Call in soon at the

Cash Store, Miss Davis. We could discuss a reduction on that lay-by of yours.'

When she wrote her article Ina strayed from Tom's information on only one point. Where he had put himself last in the order of worthiness amongst those in the hall, she promoted him to very near the top of the column. And why not? He was the retiring mayor's only son.

Tom Stocks seemed to her to be exactly the kind of person she needed to know. His hair was neatly parted, his collar and cuffs were rigid with starch, the creases in his trousers looked sharp as knives. And he smelt wonderfully of hair oil and ironing. Perhaps he was a bit dumpy in build but she imagined that would turn, with maturity, into mercantile solidness.

TEN

He sat on the ravaged carpet with his back against the corridor wall. On either side the closed doors and the rows of lamps stretched away. Above his head steam whispered in the pipes.

He wasn't certain but it could have been in this wing, in one of these rooms, that Ina passed on to him the burden of her life story. Perhaps in the room directly opposite, behind that particular closed door, she had set the whirring going in him. He would never know the exact room, that was obvious from the labyrinthine vastness of the building. He felt a great temptation to decide on one room and say, 'That was it', but some most moral part of himself rejected the idea.

Resting against the wall, his head spun with questions. Why had Ina's history taken root in him, tainted him, lain in him, driven him? Why hadn't he simply forgotten? It was typically Australian to forget history. A march and a booze-up every autumn was enough History for the nation (so the thinking went); a few snapshots in a trunk under the house enough for any family. We bury History here, mate. To get rid of the stink.

The Great Australian Forgetfulness, he had discovered, was a concept older than white Australia. It was predicted in the fourteenth century that Australia would be the Lethean land. One of the earliest imagined versions of the antipodean continent was Dante's Purgatory—the land on the other side of the known world—where the River Lethe sprang. John had unearthed this by accident when he had written an assignment on 'Town Planning in *The Divine Comedy*' in his honours year at university. It was a self-chosen topic—satirical—meant to demonstrate the hellishness of cities. It had earned him a distinction.

Like most Australians, he supposed, he had lived in a vacuum of forgetfulness. History that he had called his own was limited to the most superficial personal memories, the family photo albums and home movies and the few repeated family stories. In a country devoid of traditions there was no need for memory. The rising sun badge on the Australian soldier's slouch hat said it all: We live for the day. We don't root around in the dark dusty cupboard of the past.

Even the newly fashionable genealogists sold only names and dates. Nothing too substantial or threatening.

Sitting in the condemned maze of the Hydro's corridors, John wanted much more than genealogy. He wanted flesh and blood. He wanted the madness of Ina's thinking. He wanted to dance with the stink of corpses. That was the corruption which had danced in him all his life and he had not known it until it was too late.

He wanted the full hell of memory: the Ina within himself and the Francis within Ina. Alive.

35

ELEVEN

Ina married Tom Stocks at the end of 1911. He was twenty-five. She was still sixteen, but no one in the Stocks family ever found out. She said she was twenty-one. All her family were in Europe, she told them. She gave a list of bogus names and addresses in France and Italy for the invitations to be sent to. None of them came back, none were responded to.

'It's the political situation over there,' Big Tom nodded. 'We'll look after you, girl.'

There was no one seated on her side of the church at the wedding. She allowed it to be entered in the marriage register at St John's that she was born in Antibes of Belgian parents (a count and countess, no less). To make the fiction stick she added a string of French-sounding Christian names to her own three-lettered one: Ina Louise Yonville de Pommeroy Davis. The Davis, she said, was her poor deceased Australian aunt's name, used for convenience. Tom's family was pleased to have an association with such blue blood. Dictating her new name to the ancient church warden, watching his pen scrape slowly around its many loops, she felt wonderfully free.

Somehow she managed that deception. As with the books she had smuggled into the outhouse, she was never found out. But her lies had consequences in that she never really settled into the Stocks family, never felt truly part of it. And the Stocks never quite managed to include her amongst themselves. They were like a team for which she was only a reserve.

The entire Stocks family lived above the Wagga Cash Store

in Fitzmaurice Street. Big Tom (as the ex-mayor was called) and Emily had the main room; Big Tom's sisters Neia and Constance had two rooms with fireplaces off the perpetually dim hallway; Little Tom and his sisters had rooms opening onto the back veranda. Beneath those rooms during the day there rose the constant hum of commerce: the ring of the cash register and the whir of the overhead canisters. On Sundays the family dressed up and stepped out of the dim rooms to sit 'in the front garden'—that is, among the potted plants on the wide deck which extended out over the footpath in front of the store. The Stocks lived entirely on that level, one floor up. Their rooms and 'garden' were a world apart from the town. Cons and Neia had not been down into the street for years. During even the biggest floods (when the Murrumbidgee River sat five feet deep in Fitzmaurice Street and odd things such as a kettle or a pair of long johns might be seen floating gently between the aisles of shelves in the Cash Store) life went on as usual upstairs. There was no shifting the older generation of the Stocks. Their world was immovable.

Ina and Little Tom spent their wedding night in the Tattersall's Hotel. The very next day Ina moved in above the store and immediately felt she was a spare cog attached at the side of the family machine which ran as efficiently above as did the business beneath. Her accommodation caused few changes. The single bed in Little Tom's room was swapped for a double bed from the bedding section in the store and double sheets and blankets were brought up. Ina had no furniture, no linen, no cutlery, no pots and pans—no trousseau at all. That was lucky because there was neither room nor need for them.

She arrived with one suitcase and saw the frowns wrinkling the Stocks' high foreheads. They were sorry for her. Neia and Cons muttered about the explosive situation in Europe and the Marxian threat. Ina did not disabuse them. She glided down the hallway to Little Tom's room holding her head at just the right height to feign a burdened, enduring dignity. She kept her darkest secret well-hidden: her father had sacrificed her. She was shunted off to her aunts because his new wife disliked her and did not want her around the new children. Perhaps Ina reminded them too much of her father's first wife who had died young.

Little Tom lifted her suitcase onto the double bed. 'Good heavens. It's light as a feather.'

'It's full,' she assured him, 'of underwear.'

He wriggled his eyebrows and made a comic, excited face. 'Good-oh.'

In the first three years of her marriage Ina worked at the *Advertiser* and played a great deal of golf. Under Walter Lumsden's watchful, bloodshot eye she cultivated a good swing and a smooth action, showed great intelligence in recovery work and developed an absolute genius for pitching and putting. Lumsden was amazed at her patience and strength. She was such a compact, accurate player. He had the feeling at times that she would slice a ball into dingo country or head straight for a sand trap on purpose so that she would not take the hole off him. He began to feel pride in his protégé. He was able not to care about his own agriculture in the rough and his mounting score card when he could see her ball sitting up invitingly in the middle of the fairway. He was in love with her. Or at least with her golf.

While the golf course became Ina's main source of pleasure, at home she combated her sense of foreignness, and the guilt it fostered in her, by creating a garden. Little Tom built a greenhouse for her in the lane beside the shop. His aim was undoubtedly to attract her attention away from the growing number of hours she spent swinging a club. In the greenhouse between rounds she nurtured exotic plants. Only 'exotics': delicate ferns of all sorts and rough-looking orchids which exploded with exquisite flower-laden spikes. She taught herself their proper names: *Asplenium this* and *Odontoglossum that*. It was a sensual pleasure for her to be behind the glass panels of the little greenhouse, in that halfway place between the broad acres of the golf course and the claustrophobia of the rooms above the store. The greenhouse was her niche, the one she never found upstairs. She sometimes busied herself there late at night while

Little Tom pored over the ledgers by lamplight in the Cash Store office.

One night he came to her there. 'What are you doing?' he asked. 'It's late.'

'Re-potting.'

Her fingers pressed earth around bulbs and roots. She had a quick, rough way with things in the greenhouse, The spectacular growth demonstrated how effective her techniques were but Little Tom had the feeling that she should treat the plants more gently.

He pushed aside a voluptuous spike of orchids and said, 'Perhaps we should be thinking about having a child.'

She did not answer immediately. The dim lamp glowed creamily in reflection in a dozen panes. Against the black of the night beyond, the two were reflected in the glass walls like monkeys highlighted in a dark forest.

'Perhaps we could put it off for a while. There'll be a district associates' championship this year. Walter says I have a wonderful chance.'

'Bloody Walter,' Little Tom cursed. 'Bloody golf. Worst lay-by I ever negotiated. Wish you'd never got those bloody sticks at all.'

She came out from the fronds which hung over her work bench. She held him as he stood unhappily contemplating his own reflection in the glass wall.

'Don't swear,' she said. 'Your father doesn't like it.'

'I'm fed up with golf. I haven't got a wife, I've got an appendage to a bag of sticks.'

She laughed. She pressed herself against him and pulled the cord to turn out the light. In the dark they grappled and clung to each other while the exotics spilled out their fragrances. Afterwards as they left, the greenhouse door closed behind them and Ina heard its creak and was reminded of the outhouse at her aunts' place, and knew she did not want to be pregnant.

In the three years after his retirement Big Tom went downstairs only once. That was on the hot, dusty day of Little Tom and Ina's wedding. For the rest he dressed each morning in the same black suits, starched cut-away collars and shiny black boots which he had worn at official functions when he was mayor. Every day he spent sprawled on the bed in the main room, on top of the quilt, propped up by pillows. He had the papers delivered and could rant for hours against the way his successors on council were running the town. Under his rage the bed would squeak imperiously in rhythm with the out-flinging of his arms and the twitching of his boots. If Ina ventured near his doorway Big Tom would rant at her:

'Can't that gutless *Advertiser* exert some pressure on these people? Don't you journalists have any civic conscience? Don't you care about what's happening in this town?'

By retiring to his room Big Tom created the impression that he had given up running the business, but the cash books and ledgers were delivered into his hands each week and the advice he offered from the bed in large quantity to his son leaning in the doorway underlay every managerial decision Little Tom made.

'Put the men's watertights on sale, boy. They reckon in the paper this drought'll hold for another year yet.'

From Ina's point of view the most influential of Big Tom's decisions occurred on Wednesday the fifth of August, 1914. It was the day when news arrived in Australia of Germany's invasion of Belgium. Ina had worked late at the *Advertiser*, she and Lumsden having forgone their midweek nine holes. In the unseasonal dustiness of the evening she had walked down Fitz-maurice Street feeling frightened and exhausted. The cables from Europe were horrifyingly graphic: she imagined hard men overrunning the earth; and the Prime Minister had already committed Australia to the thick of the fighting. She peered down the dim lane beside the Wagga Cash Store and saw that her greenhouse had been levelled. The demolishers had saved the panes of glass and much of the timber, but the lane was littered with broken pots, mauled bulbs and trampled fronds. She burst into tears in the dusty, dark street.

'War has been declared, my dear,' Big Tom lectured her from the bed as her husband stood guiltily silent, half-turned behind her, not protesting on her behalf. 'That means a boom in business,' Big Tom went on. His black suit crackled as he folded his arms over his chest. 'We're expanding into the lane to cater for it.'

TWELVE

John had in his head the image of the front page of a newspaper. The headline read: 'Australia will be there!' but the photograph showed a laneway off a main street in a dusty country town. A dotted line came around the corner and a big cross marked the spot:

————X—INA'S GREENHOUSE GONE.

Could he blame history for Francis' death? There would be relief in doing so. 'The outbreak of the war brought Ina's greenhouse down; and Ina's greenhouse falling led to Andrew, led to Vaimuru, led to Johnno, led to Francis dead of AIDS, dead of the sting in history's tail.'

He clasped the central heating pipe above his head and pulled himself up from where he sat. He rubbed his bony buttocks, trying to massage away the pain of sitting. Then he turned and began to retrace his steps through the stricken corridors, following a thin strand of recognition of features seen earlier in the morning: a bare patch of carpet here, an oddly shaped vestibule there.

John had married because of a war and a lottery.

In 1966 his marble was pulled out of the barrel of the Tattersall's lottery equipment in Melbourne and he was called up for service in Vietnam, along with all the nineteen-year-olds sharing his birth date. When he received the letter notifying him of the temporary deferment of his conscription on the grounds that he had yet to finish his university course, he noticed that the final date for *permanent* deferment on the grounds of being married was still four months away. Thinking that he had found a marvellous loophole, and that the government had made a blunder, he married before the deadline.

The girl was a student too, enrolled in a social work degree. She had a wild, humorous intellectual streak which he liked. In spite of her plumpness she always wore very tight jeans and shirts which were unbuttoned to reveal a shadowy, lolling *décolletage*. She was a distinction student. She had a natural, nervous intelligence which translated in academic terms as empathy and conscientiousness. For John it translated as sexiness.

She was willing enough late at night in the back of his father's Fairmont station wagon, though nothing of a very satisfactory nature took place there on the hard fold-down floor. They always drove to the same spot—a parking area on a headland overlooking one of Sydney's northern beaches. A row of dark cars parked side by side every Friday and Saturday night, as if at a drive-in theatre with the great expanse of dark sky looming over the Pacific ocean for a screen. When they rolled a window down they heard the breakers at the foot of the headland cliff. For John and Deborah those were times of exploration which did not go far enough; exploration of themselves more than of each other. They went to parties, to dances, to cheap restaurants, but none of it added to what they knew of each other from the back of the Fairmont.

John approached Deborah's father one Saturday afternoon. He was in the backyard, digging in the vegetable garden, surrounded by tomato plants. A droplet of sweat swung at the tip of his nose. 'What is it?' he grumbled, not wanting to be interrupted.

John had difficulty speaking in spite of his rehearsals. 'I've come to ask for your daughter's hand in marriage.' Quavering, nervous. Both men were embarrassed.

'I don't care what she does,' the father said. 'She does what she likes. She's a grown woman.'

They stared at each other, exasperated by the ridiculous ritual. Then John turned back along the staked rows, knowing Deborah was waiting inside the house with her mother able to hear her father's voice follow him:

'Perhaps Vietnam would be preferable. I had quite a good time during the war years myself.'

John stopped, but did not turn around. 'I don't want to kill anyone.'

He heard the thud of the spade. 'You don't have to be in combat. I was in Supplies. Hardly touched a gun.'

'I don't want to be responsible for killing anyone.'

Her father snorted. 'You think marriage won't kill the two of you?'

Something in John was wounded. 'We get on really well together,' he shouted, and blindly moved on.

The marriage lasted five years. It was characterised not by Long Tans or Tet offensives, but by lack of engagement. John and Deborah did get on well but not profoundly; the absence of friction was due to absence of contact. Marriage did not bind them, it simply put them on parallel paths. In his head John found the need for his own downtown Saigon—his Tu Do Street—where he visited fantasy bars and could pretend he was a thousand miles from the marriage front. He spent a lot of time in the toilet looking at magazines.

After graduation Deborah took a job as a social worker with the child welfare department, yet it was John's growing view that there was no one more lacking in heart-felt empathy. In marriage she seemed to clam up. The promise shown in the back of the Fairmont did not develop. A phantom door shut somewhere between them in their first year together. In an odd way he felt that he was still in the station wagon but she was outside in the night: he could see her through the window, out of reach.

She grew silent, secretive, self-contained. He supposed it was because of his trouble with sex, his premature ejaculations, an adolescent eagerness which persisted to annoy and frustrate him.

'It's a common enough problem,' he told her, reassuring himself too. 'I'll get over it.'

He tried thinking at the critical moment of the least sexually-arousing idea possible. And what came to his mind every time, strangely enough, was a moving picture in silent slow motion of his mother descending the backyard steps carrying a tray in her hands. It drew him back from the brink. The discovery also led him to realise that it was not Deborah herself who aroused him but his fantasy of her. He was urged towards sex by a picture of her in his head, not by the touch or taste, or even the sight of her. Generated from within, his passion collided with her body but he never lost himself in her. He had his deepest orgasms masturbating with girls in centrefolds.

As he grew aware of the barrier between himself and Deborah, he also realised that she did not seem to mind it being there. She made no complaint. She appeared satisfied with her life, her job, her marriage. She grew fiercely self-righteous when pressed to talk about them. She displayed no ambition to change things.

They never argued. They never shouted things out. They never cut into each other to discover what was there. She worked in the day and would come home exhausted. Often she went to bed early, too tired even to bother to say goodnight, which irritated him hugely. He did much of the study for his Master's thesis at night, and woke up after she had left for work. On weekends she had her quiet friends over. They all worked in the welfare sector. They sat at the kitchen table and spoke intensely of women's refuges and rape and the brands of herbal tea they drank.

He knew something was tragically wrong when he realised she bored him. He saw it first at a party when he noticed she was the most sober person there, and unaccountably he felt humiliated. A party rich in jokes, in back-slapping, in witty exchanges, in boozing—and she was the death of it in his eyes. She sank beneath the waves of merriment and he felt himself being dragged down with her. After that, there was nothing about her that did not increase his dissatisfaction. It was only at the end of those five years that he discovered she too, in marriage, was avoiding a Vietnam.

Finally John needed to break a few bonds. Student theatricals gave him his chance. He saw a notice in the university union announcing auditions for a melodrama production in a local hall. He had never acted before but neither had some of the others. In a most successful first role he played the villain's off-sider—a gullible comic idiot. He revelled in the audience reaction; they laughed and applauded. His second role had him in a straitjacket for the entire play. It was Peter Weiss' *Marat-Sade*, and Freeman was cast as an asylum inmate and ex-priest, Jacques Roux. The most challenging aspect of the part was for him to keep a long rope of saliva constantly swinging from his lips. He managed it, horrifying and astounding the audience. Two hours of dangling saliva each night for a week was thirsty work. At the end of it he had lost nine pounds in weight. He laughed then, standing on the bathroom scales, feeling the energy had been well spent.

During rehearsals for *Marat* he thought he fell in love with the woman who played Charlotte Corday. When the production went up his own performance was lifted by the constant sight of her marvellous dark-nippled tits joggling behind the see-through blouse of her costume. Apart from feasting his eyes, he did not dare approach her in any way other than the metaphysical. He did not dare ask her, 'Would you like a cup of coffee?' but he fantasised about her in bed at night. His lack of confidence he attributed at first to the stifling effect of his too early marriage. But he became convinced of something more. She laughed at one of his jokes in passing and he detected a hint of condescension; she played an occasional line fiercely against his, and he noticed the ironic seductiveness in her eyes. Gradually he knew he was frightened of her.

While John was hypnotised by Charlotte, James had come up behind him like a shadow. James was the actor playing Marat— the revolutionary leader who spent the entire play in the bath, dying of a skin disease. John thought James a bore at first, as did the rest of the cast. He was of the type who boasted endlessly about himself and bitched about others. Even though John knew James was a homosexual he had no awareness that James was as desperate about the curve of his (John's) pyjama-clad bottom as he (John) was about the jutting of Charlotte's shirt. But as the rehearsals continued and John watched the rest of the cast treat James with a minimum of sympathy, he began to feel sorry for him, and just a little entertained by him too. So James latched on hard.

'Do you play golf? Why don't you play golf? Your grandmother played golf? I'll teach you. You'll love it. You can hire a left-handed set at the pro shop. I'll pay for them. Tomorrow. How does tomorrow sound?' James was lonely, John reasoned. James' passionate interest in him was the result of rejection everywhere else, John reasoned. And anyway, John was amused by him.

'Golf is all about balls in holes, John. What more delightful game can you imagine?'

James was a surprisingly good golfer, although his mincing on the greens was a source of mirth for other clubmembers, and his tendency to drop into the most embarrassing fruity accent while addressing any shot was too much even for John's sympathy. James would cry 'Ouch!' after the *pwang* of a tee-shot. He also had a self-conscious way of giggling each time he put his hand into the hole to retrieve the ball. But John saw none of this as seduction aimed at himself; in fact it had quite the reverse effect on him. Even when James stood behind him, pressing against his back and buttocks with his arms clasped around him, sighing and giggling as he gave directions in the proper grip and swing of the club, John simply laughed: James was a crazy character.

'Mmm. Your stance is *splendid*. Your swing is *stunning*. Your grip is *sensational*,' James enthused.

And John grinned. He liked James playing James. It was his best role. And he was a good teacher too. James taught him to play acceptable golf during the last four weeks of rehearsals. But though the teaching was good, the student failed to pick up the subtext of the game. Or refused to.

There was a backstage party on closing night after the final performance of the play. They all drank black velvet, which someone said was the quickest way to get pissed and the modern tradition in the theatre. They scribbled 'love' on each other's copies of the script and hugged and kissed, lowering each other down from the stressful heights of Thespianism.

'Darling, you were wonderful.'

Trying to ignore the voice of James at his side, John gulped down drinks and watched Charlotte through the cigarette smog and the crowd. She was out of costume now, dressed in high leather boots and a fur jacket, her heart-stopper thighs bold in leopard-skin tights.

'She should have a whip,' James sneered.

She leant back against the incline of a stepladder. Some fellow John had not seen before hovered beside her, dangling his long scarf against her.

'He's doing a doctorate in Psychology,' James whined. 'How boring can you get?'

John turned away. The black velvets were lined up in paper cups along a trestle table. Someone was still pouring them. He took up one and drank it down, then took up two more.

'You were so well-hung tonight, John dear. Your dangle was divine. I never saw such potent saliva...'

John moved away. He went down the passageway to the toilet. He closed the door and flicked the switch, but the globe had gone. In the darkness he relieved himself inaccurately, jumping when he felt the warm splash against his shoes. *Fuck it.* It was funny as hell, but he couldn't laugh at it.

'Goodbye, Charlotte,' he thought.

At the hall side door in the early hours of the morning, James invited John back to his flat. John was too drunk not to say yes to the first invitation he received, especially since he had seen Charlotte's tits drive off in the long scarf's Triumph. James took him to his place in Glebe. A wire screen door. A narrow dinginess. In a miasma of stout and champagne fumes and more glasses of flagon wine, John sat at the wobbly kitchen table and heard James tell stories of his childhood ballet lessons, his being raped by two women when he was twelve, his failed ambition to be a dancer, his rejection by his schoolmates...

While John was feeling an appropriate drunken sympathy he saw the record player on the sideboard being opened and the hole in a disc being fitted onto the tall spindle in the middle of the turntable and the support arm being brought across. Then the turntable began to whirl and as his head whirled with it, the record fell with a sudden clatter, the playing arm cranked itself up, jerked, plunged over the record. When a classical piece emerged scratchily from the speaker, he looked around at another set of movements and saw James in dance shoes and awkwardly bulging tights in the middle of a patch on the worn carpet dancing jerkily on his toes, spreading himself out in a wobbly, determined arabesque, energetically whirling and puffing.

Confusion galloped in his head. His thoughts rioted as James danced for him, as James threw himself into the dance. And from the whirling man there flew sparks of seduction, of hungry, desperate craving, of intimate need. His entire consciousness, spinning with drink, was challenged.

Then, in only the time it would have taken for his father to change a spool on the home movie projector, he was looking at the empty space on the worn carpet and hearing James call him from the bathroom. He felt his body standing up, pushing against the table, threading its way from the kitchen. He swayed towards the call, down the dark hallway to the lighted doorway. He found James in the bath with a backdrop of primitive gas plumbing. And with the bathroom whirling about him he gave to James the *coup de grâce*—a blow as unfair and as ugly as that Charlotte had delivered earlier in the night to Marat in his bath. He lurched, grabbed the plumbing above James's nakedness to save himself and opened his mouth. From his throat came a shower of laughter. Yet he knew enough of what he was doing to be alarmed at the nervous deception in the laughter—at the lack of true scorn in it. And he felt in his own nakedness, hidden under his clothes, under his fear, an awareness of a revolution kindling there, or at least of an unanswered question which no amount of laughter could drive away.

Then he walked out. There was a dotted line from the flat leading out into the street, and at the bathroom door there was a big cross:

X—JAMES LAST SEEN HERE————

THIRTEEN

John found his way back to the lounge and was surprised to discover it was lunch time. He had no appetite, but in the past five months he had realised it served him best to appear as normal in his habits as possible. In normality lay deception. He selected a bean sprout salad with juice—a dead giveaway that he was concerned about his health, but who wasn't these days?

There was a vacant table beside one of the large windows. He carried his tray to it. He had a sudden desire to sit with the precipice plunging away in front of him beyond the pane. He sat and removed the plastic wrap from the salad. Then he leant over and placed the tray on the seat opposite. As he settled himself and turned to take a look at the gaping grandeur of the view, a dark head appeared above the plank on the scaffolding outside, separated from him only by the membrane of the glass, but in an entirely different world, a world of tearing wind and danger.

The workman clambered onto the scaffold planks, turned and drew up a piece of formwork board handed to him from below. The board was almost as large as the window itself and was difficult to handle in the wind. The workman took out a sanding-block from the pocket of his shorts and began to sand down the edges of the board. He did this for several strokes, then stopped. From his shirt pocket he produced the makings for a cigarette. 'Drum' brand. John was so close he could see the individual strands of tobacco in the man's palm. He rolled and lit it, bending his shoulders forward, trapping the formwork board against the scaffold pipes with his knee, using it as shelter from the wind. He took his time, both in the making and the smoking of the cigarette. He made it seem a considerable pleasure in spite of the trying circumstance of his crouched posture.

John felt desperately uncomfortable at such a close view. He felt he was peeping improperly at an intimate act. He wanted to push his chair back to avoid touching the man, avoid breathing his odour. The workman took no notice of him; he inhaled his cigarette hunkered down behind the formwork board with the wind grabbing the cigarette smoke the moment after he exhaled it. The formwork board blocked out John's view into the gorge almost entirely. He could see only two triangles of sky at the top of the window, and a section of cliff edge down in the left-hand corner between the squatting workman's dark legs. John felt claustrophobic, nauseous.

Then, as if suddenly warned, the workman turned towards the window and caught John watching. Seeing the guilt in John's eyes, he winked. A great comic, exaggerated wink. 'Caught you,' it said.

John abandoned the salad and walked outside. Breathing heavily, he took the steps down from the landing overlooking the gorge to the beginnings of a stumble-footed path beneath the brink of the cliff on which the Hydro stood. From this position, looking up, the building's madness was apparent. The facade towered upwards from the cliff edge but the cliff itself receded below its lip where the wind had carved whorled caves in the yellow sandstone. At its outermost edge the building was supported by rock which was in turn supported by nothing. Attempts had been made in places to shore up the overhang with piers, but the work appeared old and inadequate. John knocked at one of the piers and dislodged a piece of cement.

To shelter from the clawing wind, he sidled into one of the cave-like depressions. His body still heaved with the unease left by the incident with the workman. He pressed himself against the rock face. Its surface was gritty to the touch. The wind's carving had produced on it marvellous yellow-banded configurations, like the pressure gradients on a meteorologist's map. As he leant against the cave wall he felt his shoulder dislodge another sandy layer of the Hydro's foundation. He shuddered at the guilt of it, brushing the coarse yellow sand from his coat. By such fine layers, he realised, the world had been forever wearing away.

FOURTEEN

The decision to extend the Wagga Cash Store into the lane proved, in the first year of the war, to be totally unwarranted. No military training camp was established at nearby Albury, as had been mooted; the drought persisted; much of the rural working population marched off and enlisted so business fell away rather than increased. With such an extended family to support from the store, Big Tom decided that the load had to be lightened. Through a business contact in Sydney he found Little Tom a position in the tobacco industry for the duration of the war.

'It might not be as glorious as Gallipoli,' Big Tom said. 'Still, it'll keep us solvent.'

'But I don't know anything about the tobacco industry. I don't even smoke.'

'Well *start*, son. Get downstairs and help yourself to a tin full. Let me recommend Players Extra Cut.'

The job in Sydney could have been classified 'Essential' had classification been introduced at that time: Little Tom was to manage a cigarette-making factory. Ina resigned from the *Advertiser* knowing that she would have had to do so even if they had not been moving to Sydney. She was four months pregnant.

Ina and Tom drove to Sydney. The road was furrowed and potholed, baked dry by the drought, and treacherous with dust-drifts. She held her stomach the entire way. Other vehicles tossed up dirt and dried manure in their wakes, while fresh manure spattered around the fenders. Little Tom drove furiously: she knew it was because of his guilt at not enlisting. Near

Gundagai they passed a ragtag procession of men (all volunteers marching to Sydney to join up) who called to Little Tom, 'Coo-ee, mate.' He hunched down behind the wheel as he overtook them, a cigarette dangling nervously at the corner of his mouth.

In Sydney Little Tom and Ina set up in a nice house in Haberfield, rented out by a doctor who had volunteered with the Anzacs. Tom drove to the factory each day and found the work to his liking. He smoked a great deal to indicate his faith in the factory's product and he encouraged Ina to do so too. Those who visited the Haberfield house received free cans of cigarettes. In every drawer or cupboard, in every crevice of the car, there were cigarettes. Tom quickly became an expert in the appraisal of tobaccos. 'You don't have to smoke a cigarette to know if it's any good,' Ina often heard him say. 'You just listen to it.' In one of her enduring memories of him he stood, with his head slightly tilted, gently rolling a factory-made cigarette between thumb and forefinger beside his ear. 'It's the texture of the tobaccos—the moisture content and the cut—that's what you hear.'

Ina was admitted to the Sydney Women's Hospital two days before the arrival of their daughter Louise. On the morning of the birth Little Tom drove through Ashfield on his way to the hospital and copped an egg in the side of the face. He turned his head quickly enough to see a young woman disappear behind a closing front door under a veranda. Forgetting Ina and the baby, he swerved to the side of the road and stopped. He got out of the car, wiping the mess from his ear and from under his collar with a handkerchief. He opened the front gate of the woman's house and stepped onto the veranda. He knocked angrily at the door, but there was silence inside the house. He waited, and noticed a neighbour emerge onto the veranda next door.

'Who lives here?' he demanded.

The neighbour was an old man. He looked at Little Tom pulling at his gluey collar, still dabbing at his vest with his handkerchief.

'She's got a husband at the war. Or she did have.' The neighbour stared at Little Tom accusingly.

'Well, I'm doing my bit,' Little Tom shouted. 'Somebody's got to make the bloody cigarettes the boys all smoke. Or do you want the whole country to close down while we all go to Gallipoli?'

The old man soaked up his anger like a sponge. 'I never threw the egg,' he said. 'And Mrs Wellings didn't really throw the egg. She's lost a husband, hasn't she? You could say he threw the egg. Or blame the Empire, why don't you? Blame the King himself, and Mr Hughes to boot!'

Little Tom slammed the gate and got back into the car. His heart was pounding and he felt the blood pricking his face.

At the hospital, standing at the end of Ina's bed, he handed out cigarettes to the nursing staff and praised the Turks, in all fairness, for their excellent tobaccos. He was over-excited. To Ina it looked like fatherly pride and nervousness. In a passionate voice he told a story which had passed through the industry: about an Aussie soldier and a Turkish soldier who met on a ridge above the Cove. They bobbed up from their trenches and approached each other during an armistice. They exchanged cigarettes, smoked them, indicated by hand-signals and head-nodding that they were both well-pleased with the swap, then went back to their trenches and reluctantly had to start firing at each other again once the armistice was finished.

'What do you make of that, eh?' Tom asked the slightly bewildered nurses. 'Doesn't that put cigarettes above war and King and Empire? And doesn't it make the Aussie job equal to the Turkish? Perhaps better?'

The story gave Tom a small feeling of revenge, though his audience could hardly realise why. He stubbed out his cigarette in an ashtray then looked at the bed, seeing Ina and the child at last.

FIFTEEN

John's first job after leaving university was with an inner city
municipal council. He was placed in an office with two architects, Rodney and Doug. Although they were young men still
in their twenties, Rodney and Doug operated with a cynicism
which surprised John at first. Rodney had a freelance design
business and blatantly drew up plans on government time and
paper. Doug was renovating his house and could turn a day in
the field on council business into a profitable hunt for his own
building materials. They were expert public servants.

'You're in luck,' Rodney said on John's first day at his desk.
'This week we're designing a dunny. Very important dunny.
Most popular meeting place in the ward.'

'It'll need over-sized cubicles for the homosexuals,' Doug
mused, 'and extra wide urinals for the police.'

'Or vice versa.'

'How about plush seats and a mirrored ceiling.'

'Or picture windows.'

'Strobe lighting. Performance stage.'

'Let's make it high rise.'

'Multifunctional. Mens, Ladies, Others.'

'Give it a back entrance, then—'

John had a dislike of public toilets. He had never been able
to tell his parents about the man who had followed him once in
the Botanical Gardens. Johnno had gone into the Gents on the
way to his weekly music lesson and the man had emerged from a
cubicle. The man had not done anything except stand close

behind Johnno, watching him piss. When Johnno left, the man followed.

John would never forget that figure—a man in a grey suit and hat, with a grey overcoat draped over his arm: completely ordinary, yet menacing. Johnno had run through the Gardens past the picturesque statues of Peter Pan and Captain Cook, past the bright display of the floral clock and the serene goldfish ponds. He had run for all he was worth to escape an ordinary-looking man who wouldn't take his eyes off him.

At the exit gate Johnno had turned around and seen the man still coming, walking at a steady, ordinary pace, way back along the path between the trees. Then Johnno had plunged across the road and into the Conservatorium where, due to his nervousness, his piano lesson that day was a disaster.

'Something Gothic,' Rodney suggested. 'Gargoyles in the urinal.'

'Something lavish,' Doug quipped. 'Fart Nouveau.'

'I've got it,' John said. 'Something comfortable but not too friendly: the Bauhaus Shithouse.'

Rodney and Doug laughed, concurring with the new town planner's first ever professional suggestion.

SIXTEEN

John went back to his room. He needed to rest. But before he lay down on the bed he ran a hot bath. He lay in the water and soaked, knowing it was dangerous to do so but enjoying the heat of it. If it was likely to give him pneumonia, he only cared in the way a soldier at the front cared about the news of a likely enemy offensive. He deflected it, he added it to the store of fear in the rear compartment of his mind. On the door of that compartment was the sign: EXPLOSIVES. He tried to keep that door locked.

Seeing his narrow body before him in the water he remembered how, as a young kid in the bath, he used to push his genitals down between his legs and clasp his thighs together over them so that just a vacant V showed. By that he could tell how he would have looked if he had been a girl. *If I'd been born a girl, I'd have been thus depleted. Or thus enhanced.* It was a strange thing to do; he recognised that even then. He had no idea whether other boys did it.

And he had no idea whether others remembered childhood as he did: in fierce flashes. Some incidents he recalled subjectively (from inside his head, so to speak) seeing them again as he had seen them at the time. Others he had somehow managed to record objectively, viewing himself in action in settings as if he watched a film.

Thus he could conjure in his mind the shapes he saw in the stone flagging on the patio of his parents' house, or his view of the man in the Botanical Gardens, or the rock ledge where Graeme Thorne lay. Thus also he saw himself standing against the wall at Seaforth Primary, his feet the shooting target for two

bullies with an air gun ('Okay, Freeman. Let's see you dance.').
Or he saw a boy dive into the shadowed depths of the floodlit
pool at the Hydro and knew the boy to be himself.

Although his memory lacked apparent discipline, it operated
with consistency in one respect: his recall of anguish was perfect, it seemed.

After the disturbing evening with James, John faced up to a
process of self-examination. It wasn't just a look at the outside
of himself, as with the boy-girl in the bath routine; it was a long
and alarming look inside. Alarming first because he knew of no
family precedent for what he had begun to suspect. Alarming
also because, like most Australian boys, he had grown up in the
cult of the Australian male as red-blooded poofter-basher, and
this naive view had settled in his mind a fear of the whole
question of being homosexual. Yet, as the ironies unfolded for
him, he began to see much of Australian male culture, especially mateship and its implied chauvinist misogyny, in a different
light. What other culture in the world, he had wondered,
placed so much emphasis on male friendship, on fierce mascu-
line loyalties, on a national cult of ignorance of women and yet
insisted that there was not one iota of male-to-male sensuality
involved?

Shoulder to shoulder together in the trenches of war and
industry by day, winking and cheering in the messes, clubs and
pubs by night! A few beers, a feed of steak, and a flamin' good
Indian arm-wrestle—come on, mate! But not a word to the old
enemy, the boss, the prison warder, the headmistress—you
know—the missus! Bugger her!

Simply by indulging in a conscious process of self-examination John felt disqualified from the Australian brand of man-
hood. You looked in the mirror behind the bar to admire your
musculature or your tan, yes, to check what a good bloke you
were but you looked no deeper. You didn't scratch the bronzed
surface. You didn't give yourself a tap to test for termites. John
had once read in a pest controllers' manual, under the heading
A Test for Termites: 'Tap the painted surface and see if it
crumbles.'

John discovered in his period of self-examination that he was riddled with termites. Whenever he was close to another male he found himself analysing the experience of that proximity, measuring its stimulating qualities. He had to admit that the sexuality of men was just as unsettling for him as was the sexuality of women. But the men—and this frightened and fascinated him—were somehow more comfortable, less alien.

He took to looking at himself in the bathroom mirror more often, as he had done in adolescence, liking himself, being vaguely excited by his own clothed image, being very excited when naked. As a rather transparent ploy he bought his wife several raunchy skin magazines—to spice up her sex life, he insisted. She showed little interest in them but he used them himself. When Deborah was out he studied the pin-up men in the gatefolds. They reclined, erect, smiling into the camera, and he smiled back at them. He lay in bed in the dark at night, with his wife's faint snore sounding beside him, and imagined touching a man—flesh to resilient flesh—and it excited him. In the street he looked around with a new awareness pulsing from him, like a sonar, and was surprised at how many impulses he received back. Good God, was half the Australian male population homosexual? How wonderful!

But all of this was only in his head. Maybe, under stress, he thought, you could imagine your reactions in this way but it might not be a true blueprint of your natural behaviour. It was a crazy sort of exploration—attempting to discover what was natural to you. As soon as you tried to examine it, you became self-conscious about it, you selected it out, and that interfered with the naturalness.

In spite of the delights and the titillations, the process was for John an agony tantamount to turning himself inside out. In the pursuit of his true identity, his felt identity fell apart. He looked in the mirror for the face behind his face and saw his reflection—his understanding of himself—go to shards. He came out of his self-examination in a terror of confusion, but certain enough of some things to tell himself that he thought he might be homosexual.

The next inevitable step was to test the theory. He put it

off for months, simply out of cowardice. He procrastinated by trying to kindle an interest in his wife, but she had become thoroughly alien not just sexually but in everything she did. She was reduced to a featureless shadow in his environment; almost an irrelevancy. Perhaps she saw him in the same way? He suspected that was the case. Certainly there was no spark between them, and no common language any more. He took it to be an indication of the degree to which his preference had changed, or had been truthfully revealed. His wife's sexuality no longer matched his. As their two bodies lay side by side in the dark bed, he imagined a front-page photograph of a headland cliff face. A dotted line curved downwards from the carpark above and ended at two crosses on the rock shelf below:

————XX—BODIES FOUND HERE.

Then he did it.

One Saturday night he prepared to go into town without her. Leaving the house he called, 'I'll be late.' His nervousness was obvious. He heard the quaver in his own voice. She sat at the kitchen table and watched him go. He wondered if he saw a hint of panic in her eyes, as if she might have been momentarily a mother and he a son. He had the feeling that they nearly talked then, nearly came out with questions, explanations, accusations, sympathies. *She knows what I'm doing.* But the moment passed. He closed the door, drove into town and parked the car in a back street in Darlinghurst.

He sat alone in the lounge of an Oxford Street pub, drinking. His bowels churned painfully with nervousness. He got up twice to go to the Gents and tried to shit. But that did no good. He managed to laugh at himself but the panic did not leave him, and he came close several times to fleeing back to his car and the safety of home. It was the worst case of stage fright he had experienced.

When John saw the man drawing near across the half-empty lounge he wanted to fling his arms wide and welcome him. In his worst forecasting fantasies of this moment the person who approached had been entirely different, not at all to his taste. Sometimes in the fantasy it had been James—shrill, vulnerable, bristling. Other times it was one of the figures from the skin mags, a lump in leather holding out a steroid-plump fist. As it was, when the real moment came, his panic vanished. The man approached and John felt an uncontrollable smile break out on his face.

The contracts were two glasses of wine; drinking them together were the signatures. There was no wrangle, no clause to interpret, no sum to be negotiated. They sipped and said their names: Phil, John. How are you? I'm well. They laughed a little madly. In the desperate hope, tentativeness, of the exchange it was John who felt himself to be the property, the chattel; and the other man acknowledged it to be so. *He knows I'm a virgin. I expect it's obvious. God, what do you say? How do you do it?* Phil invited him back to his place, then went to telephone for a car.

John was surprised when the car turned up. It wasn't a taxi. From the Oxford Street footpath he stepped into a white stretched limousine. The grey leather seats in the back faced each other. The hi-fi system played a muted classical piece. John sat on the seat facing the rear. His partner sprawled on the forward-facing seat with a studied carelessness. When the car set off and John had the odd sensation of swooping down city streets backwards, he wondered was he supposed to do anything yet, here in the car already. Should he rub knees with the other man? Grope him? Was it a camping body in this limo? *Will I dare say that out loud?* He did.

'Is it a camping body?'

They laughed together, more than a little madly, each admitting in the laughter their shared nervousness and happiness, the mutual trepidation and hunger.

The limousine crossed the harbour bridge and John knew he began to babble then, but he could not stop himself. He told things about himself that he wished he hadn't: how he had graduated from university with first-class honours; how his first plan for a subdivision had astounded the senior men in the authority he worked for; how his most recent role in a Joe Orton play had been applauded in a suburban theatre. All this nonsense, he realised, revealed his feelings of inferiority, his sense of being a foolish boy again. It was only later that he realised the other man was saying the same sort of things: that he was an executive with a recording company; that he had produced three number one hits; that he had handled the Australian tours of several American entertainers whose names John recognised immediately. By the time the limousine reached Phil's house they were well acquainted with each other's successes—or at least with the best they had to say of themselves. And from the boasting each had learnt of the other's fear and shyness.

In bed it was the same. Lacking familiarity, they collided hungrily, without grace. In the tyranny of their passion, its frenzied grappling, its gluttony of the skin, its acute mechanics, they were engulfed and humbled. There was relief only in the humour of the snags and miscalculations, soon overcome. John gave himself to the sweep of a new tide in him. He felt himself buoyed up and suffocated, both. In his desire to impress his partner, and in the importance of forging a new image of himself, he conquered several premature ejaculations. He had control. He gave himself and received himself in a burning abundance of knowledge. After the first torrent had passed, he lay in a lather of sweat, and laughed triumphantly. It was the first time he had laughed after sex.

He did not want to leave. He did not think to himself: What am I doing here? I wish I was somewhere else. He recognised with some amusement that there was a part of him (the scientist conducting the experiment) which monitored every scrap of data throughout the evening. He knew that he was alive at a profusion of levels, as if high on a drug. And he supposed that was exactly what was happening. There was in his veins, his loins, his brain, the fiery, self-revealing drug: abandonment. He felt like an actor at last allowed to play himself. It was a splendid relief.

He stayed the night with Phil. He might have rung his wife to explain (the thought crossed his mind) but he did not care enough to do so. He accepted under the rush of the new current within that his future was suddenly and drastically changed. Sane, crazy: it did not matter. If he had rung he would not have been able to control the exultation in his voice. It would be worse for her, he figured, if he did ring. He slept.

In the light of morning there was more embarrassment than he would have predicted, and a greater sense of haste on Phil's part to be rid of him.

'You can't stay. I'm sorry.'

There was early light filtering through ivy-framed stained glass. There was a pleasant smell of rush mats. There was an air of expensiveness—ancient pottery, polished black furniture against white walls—a little like a gallery. And the outrageously complicated hi-fi system, pointedly silent now, which had played Tchaikovsky's *Sixth* on automatic replay for much of the night before.

'I'd like you to leave now.'

John didn't spoil it by hanging around or asking why. He dressed and called a taxi. *No comments. No appraisals. No post-mortems.* They parted liking each other, nervous about what they had revealed, searching for regrets in each other's eyes. *We did what we had to do. We did exactly what we had to do.*

When the taxi turned into the back street in Darlinghurst where John had left his car, he saw immediately that the vehicle had been stolen. It was a terrible shock. The space of roadway where it had been—under a lamppost, opposite a warehouse door—throbbed with unreasonable emptiness. It seemed there was a gap in reality which had precisely the dimensions of his car. He could do nothing but stare at the empty space and feel betrayed.

The taxi driver was sympathetic. He was able to call the police on his two-way radio. John paid him and waited for them to arrive.

'Make of vehicle? Registration number?'

They didn't bother to get out of their car.

'Got your licence on you?'

Through the rolled-down window they took the details.

'Between what hours did it disappear?'

They spared him the trouble of explaining where he had been during the night—an uninspired courtesy, he supposed.

'Where did you last see the vehicle?'

'Right here. Right where I'm standing.'

They gave him no reassurances. 'We'll record it,' they said, and drove off.

He stood in the lane in the space where his car should have been, looking at the litter beside the kerb: a pile of old telephone directories. Then he walked around to Oxford Street to catch a bus. In his mind the image of the empty space persisted, the emptiness more tangible than the back street itself.

X—CAR LAST SEEN HERE.

On the bus trip home he tried to sort out what he wanted to say to his wife. *'Look, I've got something to tell you.'* He had no idea whether the theft of the car made things easier or more complicated. Perhaps it would lift the heat off himself a little. Perhaps he could use it as a diversion, a screen, a way of softening the blow. *'I don't want you to get a shock, but.'* Perhaps he shouldn't mention it till later. He wanted to tell her the truth about his night, about himself. He thought he wanted to. He wanted to be honest with her, to match the new honesty he had with himself. But how do you suddenly speak meaningfully to your wife for the first time when you are about to leave her? Perhaps it didn't matter. *'Somebody's knocked off the car. It's all right. It's insured.'* Perhaps he could sort it out with her on a superficial level and be done with it. Perhaps she'd view him as another of her welfare cases, and understand. *'These things happen. There's no profit in blaming.'*

He walked up Edgecliff Road from the bus stop. Sunday morning: the city hum gentler, the traffic lighter. The street had been washed in the night. Leaves were wet in the gutters. He opened the front gate and took the three steps to the door. He used his key. He went quietly. In the bedroom he found her still asleep with one of her women friends, the covers up around their heads.

He was beyond shock. He had had all the shock drained out of him. His presence in the doorway, though silent, must have changed the light in the room, charged the ions or something. His wife stirred and woke. She looked aghast for a moment, then smiled with embarrassment. 'There's something I've been wanting to tell you,' she said. Her voice slurred with sleep.

It was good to get these things into perspective. It was a perspective, wasn't it? Just seeing them in one's mind again, just following their sequence. Splicing the memories together. John thought of the boxes full of home movies, little 8 mm reels, which his father had shot but never spliced together. Scores of them. His childhood, his family life, his growing up. A jumble on plastic strips, each a five minute fragment, each itself a series of flashing fragments: Kodak, Kodak, Kodak...Flash, flash, flash...

His father washing the car in the driveway with the new-fangled hose attachment.

His mother and father swinging in the love seat on the patio.

His father diving from the tower at the public swimming pool, disappearing in a silent splash.

His mother coming down the patio steps with beer and a glass on a tray for his father. Always for his father.

...Click, click, click. The memories whirred in him.

The bath had gone tepid. He pulled the plug and watched the water whirl down the hole. It seemed full of haste to get away. The plughole choked and gagged. Voracious gravity. John dried himself looking where the mirror cut off his gaunt reflection below the waist. To think he once struggled with diets to keep his weight down! To think how he worshipped slimness! All in the past. With bony fingers he dabbed on talcum and cologne. French, expensive, ridiculously smelly. He lifted the breath freshener to his mouth and gave the atomiser bulb a hard squeeze. Crazy, he knew. The skeleton at his toilet! *Death is coming. Soon the knock at the inner door. Must look attractive for Him.* He blow-dried his hair. Yes, he'd lost quite a lot of it alarmingly quickly. What had he read about hair somewhere? That it never disintegrated. All the hair ever buried in graves still exists. Wrapped around the bones. Wrapped around the dust of the bones. *Every single hair ever cut off me, shaved off me, fallen off me, is somewhere on earth, providing it has not been burnt. Where should I start digging? Could I find just a single strand? Where do hairdressers dump people's hair?* Even the lock of his earliest hair which his mother kept for years in the baby book was gone. Page 17: BABY'S FIRST HAIRCUT. The sticky tape attaching it to the page had disintegrated, and the hair had fallen out.

In bed he lay with the blankets drawn round him. The curtains were closed against the seeping grey daylight that hovered in the gorge under a steel wool sky. Beneath the wrap of blankets he felt a film of sweat spread over his body. Feet, thighs, chest, neck, the head beneath his hair. He lay rigid, silent, trying to detect what Death was doing.

He had lived with Him for five months now. Quite a long relationship really. Graeme Thorne hadn't lasted three days in the boot of Bradley's car, but John had lasted five months in the grip of his kidnapper. For a great part of that time he had lain and listened in the dark fearful of every symptom. One of the books on AIDS which John had read described the body as a country, the immune system as its Defence Department, and the virus as an insurgent force. But the book had the wrong perspective. He wasn't aware of any grand scale forces massing or being defeated inside himself. He didn't feel like a country. He felt like a small frightened boy. There might have been whole armies of blood cells either on the attack or being decimated all along the trenches of his body but he felt only the simple, defeating helplessness that a child feels. He lay in the dimness bathed in fear, fantasising escapes and direct hits, while his sweat dwindled into the sheets.

SEVENTEEN

After the baby there was no time for golf for Ina. By the end of the year she was advanced in another pregnancy, as if her body were responding to the mounting death toll of young Anzacs overseas and was determined to begin a repopulation programme all on its own. Tom was not impressed however. He adored his eleven-month-old daughter and he looked forward to having a son (it *had* to be a son), but as this pregnancy progressed he found his wife completely unattractive.

'It gives me the willies,' he complained one night, staring at the bulge in the front of her dress.

'It's not entirely my fault,' she responded.

But he would not be humoured. 'I can't touch you.' He turned sullenly from her profile as if he were accused by it.

From then on she kept herself well-covered, never daring to show him the translucent skin, pale as whey, or the nets of blue and red veins. Each night he thrust himself to the opposite side of the bed, never caressing her, not touching her body at all.

But in the freedom of his factory office he noticed the flatness of his secretary's stomach and the narrowness of her waistline. And while the Anzacs battled on the Western Front and in the desert, Tom lay among the boxes in the factory warehouse with Norma Sheehan at his side and realised how marvellously one could taste the blend of tobaccos in a cigarette drawn on in hot guilt straight after an illicit bout of intercourse.

Ina sensed it. She smelt sex on him as strong as the cigarette smoke when he returned home in the evenings. By a thousand nameless other ways she knew too. She knew he had a passion beyond the pregnancy, beyond the house, beyond their marriage—something as strong as golf and ferns had been for her. The idea of Tom's disloyalty did not frighten her but she could not resist the temptation of discovering whose scent it was she breathed at nights.

She decided at last to go to his factory one day. A surprise visit. With Louise in her arms she climbed heavily into the nonsmoking section of a tram to town. Men rose from their seats in deference to her swollen form. She sat uncomfortably in the clanging, breezy tram (while another passenger took the child on her knee) and told herself it was the journalist in her who wanted to find out the identity of the woman involved. She did not mean her husband any ill, she simply had to have the story. TOM AND MYSTERY WOMAN DISCOVERED IN LOVE NEST. She wanted the scoop.

She walked down Ultimo Road from Pyrmont Bridge carrying the child. She climbed the iron stairway in the ash-strewn lane beside the factory. She sat in the anteroom outside Tom's vacant office where his secretary's chair, also vacant, stared back at her. She heard the thump of the machinery below and inhaled the sweet rich odour of tobaccos. Then she heard footsteps ringing on the stairs outside and waited for the door to open.

That was the first she saw of Andrew Prideaux: a sun-tanned hand, then a cream suit cuff coming around the edge of the door. He walked in. He was thin and tall, with black eyes and a black moustache under a solah topee. He sat in the straight-backed chair next to Ina and stretched out his legs. They reached almost to the absent secretary's desk. Ina classified him immediately as 'an exotic'.

They were to wait ten minutes for Tom and his secretary to return. In that time they struck up a conversation. As he spoke, Prideaux made comical faces at Louise. She hid from him in her mother's skirts.

'Actually, I'm on furlough from the war in New Guinea,' he said. 'Well, it isn't much of a war, really. Nothing like the European mess. I was in the Expeditionary Force sent to Rabaul. We simply strolled in and occupied it. The worst part was: most of us were suffering from the measles. I'd been one of the few to avoid it, was having a marvellous time. Then I came down with malaria. They sent me back here to recuperate. I'm over it now. Except for a ten minute bout at seven o'clock each evening, regular as clockwork. Can tell the time by it.'

She smiled.

Prideaux looked about impatiently. 'I wonder where this Mr Stokes has vanished to.'

'Stocks,' Ina corrected. 'Tom Stocks.'

'Yes. Where is he, I wonder? I'm in rather a hurry.'

Prideaux got up and paced the office. He patted the restless child's head, glanced surreptitiously at Ina's belly, then went out the door and down the stairs.

When he appeared again in the doorway he said, 'Even the foreman doesn't know where he's got to.'

He squinted at Ina and pulled at his moustache in a puzzled way.

'Look,' he said, 'I apologise for asking, but are you waiting for Stocks too?'

'I'm his wife,' she said, and he sat down as if struck by a premature bout of his disease.

Tom and his secretary returned with a cunning space of time allowed to elapse between them. The secretary came first. She did her best to cover her shock at seeing Ina. By the time Tom returned, Louise was fussing and crying, misbehaving out of boredom. Ina had to take her from the room and down to the lane to appease her. Prideaux went into Tom's office to make his proposition for starting a tobacco plantation in Papua. Tom took a hurried glance out the door at his wife in the laneway, then followed Prideaux in.

Ina did not go back up the stairs. There was no need now. She had seen the ribbon of shredded newspaper clinging to the back of the secretary's dress as she sat down at her desk and its incriminating mate dangling from Tom's trouser cuff. They used shredded newspaper as packing in the warehouse. IDENTITY OF MYSTERY WOMAN REVEALED. Forensic Evidence Conclusive.

Ina waited at the tram stop with a strange hollowness inside her. She was more angry than she had expected. She breathed hard with the anger, and the hard breathing knocked against the lump in her stomach. The anger was not directed towards Tom or his secretary but towards a claustrophobic sense (suddenly present in her mind) of a familiar door closing against her. She did not want to be trapped again in the outhouse.

After she arrived home she lay on the bed with Louise asleep beside her and felt the violent kicking of the child inside. She considered her options, and the price she would have to pay.

The two men hit it off. Tom agreed to show Andrew Prideaux the workings of the business over the next weeks. He put in a good word for Prideaux with the company director, whom Prideaux approached for financial backing. Tom declared Prideaux to be a natural for the industry: he had an instinctive feel for tobaccos and he had a voracious appetite for learning about them. One night in the first week of their acquaintance Ina watched the two men holding cigarettes at their ears, rolling them between finger and thumb, listening intently.

'What are you two doing? Trying to call long distance?'

'Don't interrupt, woman.'

From the kitchen where she stood, big-bodied, legs apart, she could not resist comparing them. There was a sturdiness to Little Tom, a stocky sort of gravity—a force which took others with it. But Andrew Prideaux was volatile, charged with an electricity, a quickness. That was how they seemed to her. One was earth, the other fire.

'We're listening to the sound of money.'

'How it's going to rustle in Papua.'

She had the feeling that there was something calculated in Little Tom's new friendship with Prideaux. He was using Prideaux as a screen to hide his guilt from her, she thought, and this was a further complication of the fact that he was using Norma Sheehan, his secretary, as a screen to hide his guilt about the war from himself.

Tom put the cigarette into his mouth and lit it. He blew a quivering smoke ring. 'Why don't we have a party? Tomorrow night. To celebrate the Papua venture.'

Prideaux laughed. 'That's a bit premature. I won't be ready to go for months yet.'

'What do you reckon, Ina?' Little Tom persisted.

She felt the weight of her flesh bearing down between her legs.

'I reckon,' she said.

They got in bottles of beer and whisky, a cake from a shop, sliced meats, glacé fruits, bon-bons. Tom invited some of the staff from the factory, and drove several suburbs to pick Norma up. Ina struggled in the kitchen with plates and table cloths and cutlery and nippled bottles of milk.

'What's happening in here?'

It was Andrew Prideaux emerging from the smoke-filled living room where Little Tom was tossing Louise up towards the ceiling, and catching her, showing her off.

'I'm turning into a turtle. The kitchen's my shell.' She raised an eyebrow at his comprehending frown. 'Tell that man not to toss the child so. She's just eaten three cupcakes.'

Ina turned to the bench where the next round of plates was waiting. She felt two hands slide around her waist and grasp the globe at her front.

'Some turtle,' Andrew said in her ear.

Then the hands departed. Her own hands shook as she carried the laden plates to the party's epicentre, the dining table which had been shifted to the middle of the living room. Putting them down unsteadily, she was aware again of her bigness, only four weeks off her time her doctor had calculated.

'Here's to Papua,' someone cheered. 'To success.'

'And here's to the next one,' Little Tom shouted, throwing an arm around Ina's shoulders, the first they had touched in weeks.

'And to the boys in the Middle East,' Andrew called, raising a whisky high.

They all drank to hope and life and victory. In the midst of it Ina felt her options narrowing.

After the party, while Tom was away driving Norma home,

Andrew carried Ina across the bedroom threshold as if he had just married her. In the dark he ran his hands and face all over her belly and entered her from behind, clutching the child in her as he laboured, and she found an unaccustomed profound pleasure in it which rocked her like bomb blast. To her later alarm, she found the medical danger of it to be an aphrodisiac. And when she called out she woke Louise; but she did not care about that either. As they lay together exhausted, tingling with the fear of Little Tom's imminent return, Andrew said:

'Your husband's wrong. It's no use just listening to tobacco. You've got to use every sense your body possesses. Smell, taste, feel—the whole works.' Then he laughed. 'Really, to know a good tobacco you've got to make love to it.'

Ina's second child was born two weeks premature. Driving home from a picnic at The Spit, Tom misjudged the width of a space between a tram and a gutter at Neutral Bay Junction. One side of the car ran up onto the footpath. Ina, who was sitting in the rear, fell forward and bumped her stomach against the back of the seat in front of her. After resting on the bench at the nearby tram stop for ten minutes she felt well enough to continue. Louise, sitting beside her, was thankfully unharmed. But the child travelling inside her had another view of events. He decided it was time to bail out. On the car ferry steaming away from the vehicular wharf at Milson's Point Ina felt a convulsion inside and knew that something was happening. In the middle of the harbour her waters broke. She told Little Tom as calmly as she could, and he panicked.

'Good Christ, woman. Did you have to do it here?'

He yelled at her. He yelled at the other drivers in their vehicles jammed on the ferry deck. He yelled up to the captain in the wheelhouse. He watched wildly as his wife heaved on the back seat of the car.

'What do you want me to do? What am I supposed to do?'

When the ferry berthed he drove like a demon up Macquarie Street, blasting the horn.

'Emergency. Emergency for Christ's sake.'

Lurching on the back seat, trying to keep a hold to prevent herself and Louise from being thrown completely from the car, Ina had an experience unmatched in her nightmares.

'Tom, slow down! Please, slow down.'

Her words were lost in the car's swerving progress, in the frantic hoot of the horn, in the rush of wind under the flapping side curtains, in the uncontrollable growl and howl and gulping in her own throat. By the time Tom screeched to a halt outside the Women's Hospital, Ina and Louise and the new child were a sodden and complicated mass entwined together on the floor part way beneath the back seat.

She never forgave him. *It took five years off my life, Johnno.* She never forgot how his panic was for himself, to save himself. *Not for me or your mother.* In the shock of it all, it seemed the new child was not hers. It was the product of an accident. And just as Tom could never quite get the smell of the birth out of the car, so she could not forget the harm he had done. She lived with it for more than a year, she tried to ignore its enormity, but it shifted her at last. She had a three-year-old daughter, yes, and an eighteen-month-old son, and she left them. *I played from the fourth tee onto the fifth fairway, and I just kept going, Johnno. Simple as that. And everyone hated me for it. Except Andrew, of course.*

In the Haberfield backyard a vine arbour was built out from the rear of the house. She and Andrew sat opposite each other in cane garden chairs. His long frame was unfurled towards her, his boots touched her shoes. On his face the shade of the vine moved.

'Will you come with me to Papua, then?' he said. 'It's tomorrow I'm sailing.'

'You know I'll go anywhere with you.'

'And the children?'

'He wants them. Why shouldn't he have them? They're his.'

She watched the slide of the afternoon sun receding up the weatherboards of the outhouse further down the garden.

EIGHTEEN

John's reaction to the discovery of his new sexuality and the break-up of his marriage was to apply for several positions as a town planner, all in exotic locations: Suva, Hong Kong, Port Moresby. Port Moresby wanted him, so he resigned from the municipal authority in Sydney.

He was running away, he knew that, but it was running from a context—an environment and a past. It was not running away from himself. It was not an evasion of responsibility. If the image of running was at all appropriate, it was in the sense that he was running towards himself (on a collision course, he thought) with relief, with open arms.

In deciding to accept the Port Moresby offer, he made a fortunate choice. The town was, he learnt later, a haven for a small community of Australian homosexuals who lived in un-harassed exile in the tropics.

When the plane taxied to a halt at the airport in Moresby he looked out the narrow window. Against the backdrop of low, scrubby Port Moresby hills, he saw his first Papua New Guinean—almost his first black man; certainly the first that he had had occasion to study even at a distance—a man on an airport tractor. And in the fact that it was not a white man leaning on the wheel, John suddenly realised the extent of the convulsion his life had undergone. *I have turned inside-out.* From moderate passions in a moderate climate, the tenor of his life had shifted to tropical intensities, as if the axis of his world had lurched off-centre. A shudder, not unmixed with a sense of thrill, passed through him. But when he got off the plane and

75

walked across the tarmac to the terminal, the tropical heat hit him, thick and rich, like the moist palpable air in a greenhouse. He really did imagine new limbs might spring from him, or roots pop from the soles of his feet, so potent was the atmosphere surrounding him. In the customs and immigration hall an eager Papuan official discovered a butter knife and a pack of cards in his suitcases and confiscated them. They were offensive items in this country, apparently. One was possibly an illegal weapon, the other an illegal gambling device. John did not protest. He already accepted that his new life would be ruled by an entirely new logic.

If it seemed on the one hand that he had travelled far—from one world to another—it also seemed as if things had barely changed at all. A coin had flipped over, simple as that. The face that now lay uppermost had been hidden but always there. *I'm not a different person.* A bare-footed New Guinean slid open the customs hall exit door for him. *Not adrift without moorings. I'm still a town planner, a man, a lover. Perhaps a better one in each case: more sensitive, aware.* He passed through the noisy crowd of black bodies in the airport terminal conscious of an entirely new sensation—the pungent odour of dark sweat stirred to a tropical cocktail by the myriad ceiling fans whirring overhead. *What a fortune a deodorant manufacturer might make in this country.* He dismissed that thought, but not its sequel. *Have I ever smelt so vividly before?*

There was a large black official car waiting for him outside the terminal. A sandshoe-shod, shorts-clad chauffeur smiled a big-gapped highlands grin and lifted John's suitcases into the boot. The man gave him an envelope containing house keys and an address, with instructions to have a shower and meet someone called Goffett for lunch. He sat in the back of the car and rolled the windows right down. He was driven away from the airport along Sir Hubert Murray Drive, which was a narrow strip of bitumen flanked by red dust and puddles, banana trees, the occasional Chinese-run store, and hordes of bare-footed pedestrians. As they walked and he rode with the humid wind of the car's progress in his face, John saw for the first time the lightness of black people's soles, especially on the whirring feet of a skinny boy who ran beside the road pushing a stick with a tin-lid nailed loosely at its end. John craned his neck as the car rushed past the boy, saw the ecstasy on the boy's face, the pumping spindly legs clad in shorts far too big for him, saw too that the stick with a tin-lid wheel was a car zooming on the highway, was in the boy's imagination the big black car in which John rode. Then it crossed John's mind that he was entering a country where the imagination still ruled over the material; where town planning would be as mysterious a science as sorcery.

He was driven first to a suburb of prefabricated, louvred buildings crouched under a jungly profusion of poinciana and fig and mango trees, with gangling hibiscus hedges along alignments and crotons hugging walls. The car pulled up in the damp driveway of a moist-looking prefab structure which housed four separate flats. The chauffeur carried the suitcases up a flight of wooden stairs and deposited them against the step inside the wire screen door. Then he went back to the rear seat of the car to have a sleep. John let himself into the flat, showered as instructed, and changed into his only pair of shorts and long socks. *I will have to throw away most of my clothes. They are too hot.* Then, having securely locked the door under the directions of the awakened chauffeur (whose Pidgin English John could not follow, but whose hand signals and gestures were perfectly comprehensible), he was driven towards the town, still on Sir Hubert Murray Drive, past a bustling market beside a bay, around a headland where the pale, bright sea lapped at the road's edge, along a breezy beachfront beneath massive fig trees and into the town.

It was a dazzling drive. There was dazzle off the ocean and the beach; there was dazzle off the car bonnets and windows, and shiny green foliage. In the heat he saw a splatter of a town: a collage made up of crowds swaying in the backs of open trucks under harsh sunlight, awkward low buildings, lines of women sitting on footpaths beside lines of pots and beadwork, men wobbling on pushbikes, blotches of tree-shade dotting sun-dashed bitumen, white-skinned people hurrying on footpaths where black-skinned people lay flat out asleep, blood-red splotches (expectorated betel juice) slashed across road-side posts and shop-front windows and the corrugated iron walls of the cinema.

Moresby was a town planner's nightmare. John loved it at first sight.

The car turned in beside a bayside row of palm trees and burrowed its way down a cool tree-tunnelled side street. It came to a halt outside a wooden single-storeyed building with a veranda which reminded John of an Australian schoolhouse. Attached to the wall in the shade of the veranda was a sign: PLANNING AND DEVELOPMENT: ARCHITECTS DIVISION. There was a black man dressed in grubby khaki with a bucket and mop casually washing down the spotless veranda floorboards.

The inside of the building was practically empty. A single vacant desk stood in a large gleaming room. Another desk with only a blank writing pad on it was in the next large room. *The Planning Department. Planning from scratch, it seems.* No files, no drawing tables, no plan cabinets. And the rooms seemed barely rooms at all. More like glasshouses because of the walls of louvres. It was an old colonial building, remodelled. It was polished and spotless, especially the vast expanse of brown floorboards. But it was not empty of sound: the judder of a score of ceiling fans, each on the highest setting, chopped the air into agitated nervous currents around the rooms. *My new life; with no one to receive me.*

John stood in a doorway and watched the New Guinean with the mop and bucket. The man had washed to the end of the veranda and now sat on the step smoking a cigarette rolled in newspaper. He saw the white man watching him.

'Hello, *masta,*' he said.

John said hello in return, but there must have been a hint of agitation in his voice. The man got up quickly. He took the mop and bucket to the other end of the spotless veranda and began mopping again, head averted. John looked around. He decided to call out. He could think of nothing else to do.

'Anyone home?' he shouted.

Against the noise of the ceiling fans his voice was checked

and muffled. And no one responded. *I wonder am I in the right place?* John sat on the desk and waited.

Finally another black car drew up in the compound. John went out onto the veranda. A middle-aged man in white shorts and shirt got out, puffing on a pipe as he mounted the steps. He was short and balding. He beamed a smile of welcome through teeth clamped on the pipe-stem.

'I'm Goffett.'

He crushed John's hand in his. He drew him by the clasped hand into the empty, fan-juddering rooms.

'Isn't it marvellous?' Goffett said. 'And it's all *ours.*'

'So I'm in the right place, then?'

Goffett grinned. 'If you want to make history you are. It's a mighty small pool here and we're mighty big fish.'

They turned back out to the tree-shaded veranda where the New Guinean mopped patiently. Goffett smiled and winked, pointing his pipe in the mopper's direction.

'Best cleaner boy in the service. I pulled a few strings.'

The boards were already drying where the mopping had restarted.

Goffett took John to the Papua Hotel for lunch. He was amiable and helpful. 'The first thing you need to get this afternoon is a car.'

John didn't realise that he meant *buy* a car.

'And you'll want a *hausboi*. A house boy. I'll send one over. In Badili, aren't you? Not a bad suburb. Food? I'll take you down to the Freezer. And grog, of course. We'll get you set up.'

At six o'clock that evening John sat in the oven-like heat of his bare flat with a bottle of South Pacific beer in his hand. There was a black hunk of frozen steak thawing rapidly on the laminex in the kitchen. There was a new car (a little Japanese two-door model) parked outside the window. The beer (Goffett told him) was manufactured in the security-fenced brewery just around the corner; the steak came from Irinumu Plantation just fifteen kilometres out of town; the car was straight off the showroom floor just over the hill in Boroko. Port Moresby was a small, small world.

As the dusk seeped through the uncurtained windows John watched a large cockroach come out silently from under a skirting board, heard a gecko cluck beneath the eaves, smelt the tropical mould clinging in every nook of the flat, felt the sweat roll and drip monstrously under his shirt, tasted the miraculous cold of the SP lager...and burst into tears, feeling lost as a child.

NINETEEN

John woke in the Hydro thinking of golf balls. Remember
how in the 'fifties you could cut the white skin off a golf ball
and start unravelling the guts of it—the gutta-percha of it? It
had a feel all its own: slightly sticky, resilient. The process of
unwinding the elastic strand seemed endless, sometimes you had
to come back to it the next day. At the heart of the ball, after
all the fun of unwinding, was something even more precious
than the single hundred and thousand at the centre of a rain-
bow ball: the little rubber bag containing goo. It was useless,
that bag. It was mysterious and absurd. But to Johnno Freeman
(and to all the other kids he knew) it was a treasure, valuable
for no other reason than that it lay at the end of a long,
satisfying process. Certainly you couldn't short cut that process.
If you tried to knife through the gutta-percha you spoilt it: all
you had then was a sticky mass resembling a hedgehog. There
was no alternative: you had to go through the whole unravelling
to reach the triumphant centre. But still you couldn't do anything with that bag of goo. Mostly you threw it away pretty
soon. But its apparent meaninglessness did not fool any boy of
intelligence. For there came with the unravelling an understanding (albeit very vague, perhaps only the shadow of an
understanding) that this bag of goo was indeed the heart of the
golf ball, the very principle of it, the reason for its bounce, its
speed and its far flight.

Then they stopped making the balls that way.

John could never think of the word 'unravelling' without
making an association with a childhood incident. One night

when his father was showing home movies, the leader strip came away from the pick-up reel without anyone noticing. The family sat and watched the reel through while the film steadily spewed out at the back of the projector. When Johnno got up to turn the lights back on for his father, they saw it together: the entire film laid out on the floor behind the projector table. Not in a chaos of loops, but neatly wound, as if on a ghost reel. Unravelled and rewound at one and the same time.

TWENTY

When Ina went to Port Moresby the trip was by boat. She and Andrew arrived on the wharf and their luggage was carried up the blinding track called Musgrave Street by a line of full-grown Papuan men called 'boys'. In the relentless sunlight Ina looked around unsuccessfully for a building that was not made of corrugated iron. A court house or a bank maybe? No such luck. The entire town pulsed and shimmered. It broiled in its own iron heat. It fried the eyeballs. Even the hotel they entered had corrugated iron walls which burnt at a touch. Every structure gave off a sense of impermanence, of having been carried there from a long way off and tossed together haphazardly. The place was an eyesore. The population was mainly male. In the acute ugliness of the buildings and the barrenness of the streets she saw her role immediately. Where most of the original trees had been cleared from the townsite not a single replacement had been planted. She imagined ferns and palms growing lushly in the sandy vacant allotments between the buildings. Within minutes of getting there she knew Moresby would be her greenhouse.

'My God. This place needs trees,' she told Andrew.

'Why not tobacco?'

'Real trees, for shade.'

'We'll grow tobacco tall as trees.'

They laughed, imagining a plantation in the main street. Anything seemed possible in the harsh, rich light bouncing around them.

They booked into the iron-walled Papua Hotel. From their

stifling upstairs room she looked down on the sandy street which had never known a car tyre and barely knew a hoof or a bicycle wheel. Feet were the mode of travel, even in 1919. The roads were foot-tracks mainly, and most of them petered out outside the town.

Andrew came up to her as she stood in her petticoat at the hot wooden louvres. He put his arms around her.

'Are you happy?' he said.

She leant her head back against his shoulder. His hands roved, and killed the ache in her as they had done daily since she left her children. Killed it and killed it. How she loved them killing the ache.

'I am happy.'

Their first months in Moresby turned out to be difficult. Although Andrew had financial backing to start a tobacco plantation, he could not just walk in and buy land. Officialdom intervened. The siting of the plantation was the problem. He argued with the Directors of Agriculture and Lands and Native Affairs, who argued with each other as well. Then they all argued with Hubert Murray, the Lieutenant-governor.

Andrew became excited and angry by turns. Ina loved watching it. He was like a fireworks display. Tools, charts, the right building materials were hard to assemble in such an out-of-the-way place. Orders he had made in Sydney months earlier didn't turn up. 'The war is to blame,' he cursed. 'Everyone's trying to get back on their feet at the same time.' Added to the delays were the extra costs. Prices of goods in Moresby were frightful. The government seemed determined to test Andrew's resolve by charging him double for searches, stamp duties, development approvals. To save money they moved out of the hotel and lived for a time on a converted twin-hulled canoe, hired from the nearby village of Hanuabada. She loved it. They were doing mad things. She felt she was free.

Whenever the thought of Little Tom and the children came into her mind, she erased it. Erased it and erased it. Regretted that they existed at all. Threw off the burdens of bitterness and sadness. She arranged irregular work with the newspaper, the

Papuan Times. The editor said he would take a short article of interest to women now and then, especially if it related to matters Down South, such as how a woman in the tropics might convert a stack of tea-chests into an acceptable dining-room suite, or how she could cook a fashionable dinner out of cans. In this way Ina began to occupy herself.

One of the first items of equipment to arrive for the as yet unplanted tobacco plantation was the truck. Andrew supervised its lifting off the steamer. The motor started immediately on the wharf once some petrol was poured in, and blew a large cloud of black smoke. Andrew drove the noisy, back-firing truck down Port Road with Ina beside him, and scared the hell out of a crowd of Papuans. When the fan-belt broke after just two hundred metres (it had perished on the trip on the steamer's deck) Andrew opened the bonnet, leant in, then asked Ina to remove her stocking. She had to take it off in full view of a crowd of nervous villagers. The knotted stocking proved perfectly effective as a temporary fan belt but the story that got back to the native villages went (as one of her houseboys later informed her): *A monster has arrived from the sea. It drinks paraffin. It roars out one end and farts black smoke out the other. It has a mouth which opens and the new white man shows his courage by putting his head in it. Worst of all, the monster feeds on the skin off a white woman's leg and it will not move without such food being given.*

The next morning, when Andrew went out to crank the truck up again, he found a basket of snakes' skins left on the ground in front of it. An offer of appeasement from the villagers, Ina thought it wonderfully touching.

TWENTY-ONE

John first met his houseboy in the backyard on his second afternoon in Moresby. God knows how long the man had been waiting there but when John arrived home from work and went out to the laundry, there was Maik, in shorts and his least ragged shirt, seemingly hanging by one arm from the Hills Hoist clothesline.

Maik greeted him by letting go of the clothesline and dipping into an eccentric bow—the full theatrical, curtain-call job. Then he boomed, 'You all right, *masta?*'

The white man spoilt it immediately by saying, 'Call me John.'

Maik held a note of introduction from Goffett—a *'pas tru'*, a genuine letter, Maik called it. John looked at it. It was in Goffett's handwriting all right. He read it then screwed it up.

He discovered that Maik had not eaten all day. He took him inside and made him a tomato and cheese sandwich. Maik sat uncomfortably on a chair at the table. *It wasn't the done thing, of course. It was the first time he'd been invited to eat in a white man's house.* Maik looked at the sandwich on its plate, then he looked at John. 'You got knife and pfork?' he asked, very apologetic though at the same time hinting that the white man had erred, should not have forgotten such important items. John fetched them and watched him balance them cautiously in his hands. Then Maik ate the sandwich using the knife and fork. He did it with great dignity, with an astonishing elegance, considering he had held cutlery only once or twice before, in secret, in household kitchens where he had worked, having seen it done by the *masta* and *misis* in the dining room and wishing to imitate it, perhaps parody it. But at the time John realised too late that he had forced Maik into his first 'civilised' meal, and he watched with trepidation as the man ate on cleanly, gamely, solving the puzzle of the knife and fork as he went. *I admired him straight away.*

He gave Maik a lift home in the new car. *Again not the done thing. Europeans rode; locals walked.* Maik lived over by the airport. On the way, on the main road through Boroko, Maik suddenly asked him to stop. Beside the busy road a woman carried a baby and walked with another child at her side. She had a huge string bag full of tuberous vegetables held around her forehead and hanging down her back. John drew up next to her. Maik opened the door and got out. He pulled the back of the bucket seat forward to let the woman and child into the rear seat. Except for the big smile on his face, Maik offered no explanation. John was left to understand that this was Maik's wife and kids—the family Maik would support on the ten dollars a week John had contracted to give him. The child, a girl of about five, climbed in first. She sat bolt upright on the rear seat, bright-eyed, her hands and chin resting on the back of John's driving seat. The woman handed Maik the naked baby, and tried to clamber into the small car with the large bag of vegetables. Seeing the impossibility of getting the bag into the back seat, John opened his door and got out. He took the vegetables and put them into the boot, slamming the lid down on top of them. Then he got back behind the wheel and shut the door.

They set off. The grin on Maik's face was huge. '*Em i olsem taxi,*' he said, laughing. He held his naked son proudly on his knee. John turned around and looked over his shoulder into the back seat. The woman gave him an apprehensive smile. He couldn't twist around far enough to see the little girl who was crouched against the window now. The small interior of the car filled with the pungent odour of sweat. John wanted to roll his window down, but didn't, out of politeness.

As they drove past the radio station John noticed a quick movement out of the corner of his eye. Maik had suddenly changed the baby's position on his knee. His hand had quickly gone down to form a cup below the child's crotch. John saw the stream of urine squirt into Maik's hand. He did not turn his head or look directly at Maik. He did not want to embarrass him. The white man's new car! The baby has done *pispis!* It will get on the new seat! It will get on the clean floor! John could see the glistening pool of urine riding in Maik's hand, and he could feel the man's anguish. Then he saw the movement of the hand as Maik figured out what to do with it. Maik's fingers closed over the pool, his hand went into the pocket of his shorts...and came out empty.

Once again John felt nothing but sympathy and admiration for the man. 'Have you ever ridden in a car before?' he asked, trying to sound as warm and friendly as possible.

Maik understood the question. He answered in Pidgin first. '*Nogot, masta. Tasol mi bin raun long trak long planti taim.*'

John did not understand.

'*Mi no bin wokabaut long wanpela ka,*' Maik persisted. Finally he shook his head in the negative and John understood.

But that was not the last significant event during this short car trip. Just after John had turned right, under Maik's instructions, at the bottom of the Six Mile hill, he became aware of a stirring in the rear seat. Maik's wife was saying something to the little girl, something sharp and quick, not in Pidgin but in another language. John turned his head and saw the woman leaning across the girl. He swivelled his head the other way to get a better look at the child and saw immediately, down beside his own seat, that her hand was flat against the inside wall of the car, the fingers disappearing beyond the knuckles.

John swung to the side of the road. The car lurched to a halt in the red dirt on the verge. John opened his door as rapidly as he could. Even though freed now, the girl's hand stayed where it was, crumpled against the door-post, pale-looking.

'For God's sake, why didn't you tell me?' John yelled.

The girl looked at him, fearful at the yelling. Her mother pulled the hand away. She bent the little fingers back and forth. The girl's eyes were wide and moist, but she did not cry. The mother slapped the hand away. Nothing was broken, it seemed.

John closed the door carefully and drove on. He understood perfectly why the girl had not told him her hand was caught in the door. This was her first ride in a white man's car. How was she to know it wasn't always like this? God, he cried inside at the thought of it.

He dropped the family at their house, one in a long line of shanties along a red dirt road, squalor made picturesque by banana trees and crotons. He took a single, comprehensive look at it. *Click!* A picture of a rude shelter constructed partly of flattened beer cartons, surrounded by bare earth, foot-trodden, a mangy dog skulking by the step. A picture to be carried around forever. Then he did a U-turn and drove off.

Going back down the dirt road to the highway he felt an overwhelming sense of sadness and responsibility. He had only been in the country two days and somehow he knew already that he carried on his shoulders a century of colonial guilt. What stuck in his mind particularly was that one of the few pieces of tin that made up the patchwork of Maik's house walls was a road sign. It was nailed upside-down under a windowless window but it was perfectly readable. SIR HUBERT MURRAY DRIVE, it said.

TWENTY-TWO

At seven, and in response to his own 'normality' instructions, John went to dinner. *There used to be a bell. We all used to troop down like Pavlov's dogs.* As he approached the stained-glass double doors to the dining room he recalled how they had represented a barrier in his childhood. In the 'fifties, when his family came to the Hydro every Christmas and August holidays, he had had to eat with the other children in the 'little people's' dining room, this side of the doors. *Tables full of trifles and cakes, dark port-wine coloured jellies, lashings of ice cream. I don't remember the healthier foods.* He stood now in that room where he had eaten often, where there had been white-painted chairs and tables, all of turned wood, like furniture from a fairy tale inn. Now a few nondescript lounges and standard lamps indicated it was used as a pre-dinner drinks room for functions. No, the children's dining room did not exist any longer.

He wondered about going over to the corner where he had vomited once, when he was five, and brought up his port-wine jelly. But he decided against it. There would be no mark showing, no cross.

X—BOY THREW UP HERE.

How many thousand children must have passed through this anteroom on their way to adulthood? There wasn't a single sign of them now. The linoleum, which had been bright with the rattle and scrape of children's shoes, was mute now under pile carpet. He pushed through the double doors into the 'big people's' dining room.

90

It was more a museum than a dining room. Plainly this was one area of the hotel where there had been no renovation at all over the decades. The arched, pressed metal ceiling bore the discoloration of years of log fire smoke. The bizarre decorative pieces which sat about fatly (great Art Nouveau urns, huge swans, reclining gilded faience figures), seemed to claim their positions through long standing. Among them, fragile and transient by comparison, sat ten diners in couples at separate tables congregated towards the end of the room near the open fire. *The mid-week crowd. Honeymooners? Lovers? Adulterers? All straight.*

He sat at the next table in line. The wine waitress bustled over to him with the wine list. He waved it away. 'Just a mineral water, thank you,' he told her. She turned on her heel, her beehive hairdo swaying with vexation. *I've committed the unforgivable. I've refused the wine list.* Triumphantly he felt a pang of hunger, and ordered the blandest-looking dish from the menu. A fish in a cream sauce.

During dinner in reply to his questioning, another waitress told him that the hard-pressed wine waitress (who hovered by the cash register at the door) was in fact one of the owners, Mrs West. On the basis of this information, he decided that he would, after all, order a bottle of wine. *I shan't drink it though. It will kill me.* He called her over and made his belated selection. *Outrageously expensive. One hundred per cent mark-ups. To pay for the crumbling foundations, I suppose.* Mrs West came back with a half bottle clenched like a tennis racquet in one hand and an ice bucket (empty of ice) swinging in the other. She set the ice bucket on the table and showed him the label on the bottle.

'I hear you're the owner,' he said.

She looked at him cautiously from under her beehive. *She thinks I'm about to make a complaint.* 'I'm only the licensee,' she corrected him, pouring a half-inch of golden chardonnay into his glass. 'The place is owned by a company. I'm one of the board members.'

He waved his hand to indicate that she should pour the wine without him tasting it. 'I'm interested in the history of the Hydro. My grandmother used to live—'

'Oh, yes. There's quite a lot of history here,' she interrupted, thumping the bottle into the ice bucket and bustling off towards the cash register where a couple waited.

John ate. And against his fear of the consequences he began on the wine. His taste buds had for months been unreliable, nothing tasted as it should. But tonight normality had inexplicably returned. The fish tasted like fish, the wine like wine. He had to put his fish fork down and push the wine glass away. He felt suspicious of feeling well. He dreaded the lull before the barrage.

He wanted to talk more with Mrs West, but he could tell she was not interested in him until the level in his wine glass dipped further. *Should I pour it into my pocket?* He faked a foolish move and knocked the ice bucket from the table. She bustled over with a cloth. *She's more interesting than she lets on. All that red lipstick is just hotel trade uniform.* He asked for another bottle and she softened visibly. He looked around and noticed that three of the quiet couples had finished and gone already. *To beds. To safe beds.* Mrs West returned and stood at his table. She pulled the cork of the new bottle in a less harassed way. She seemed inclined to talk now.

'Good heavens, everyone's been here. Royalty, field-marshals, film stars. Let me see, Melba, Kingsford Smith, Conan Doyle—he predicted the fire which burnt down the old Belgravia Wing. He was into spiritualism. Predicted the murder too. I could show you the room where it happened, over in the New Wing...

'Ina Stocks? I'll look her up...

'Well, the renovations are costing a fortune. Most of the place will have to be bulldozed, it was built too close to the cliff, but there's a heritage order, you see, we can't touch it, so it's all just standing for no purpose. Except perhaps to fall into the valley. I like the idea of building a facsimile, but back this way from the cliff edge. We still have all the original plans. But it would cost so much.

'There are masses of photographs. I could show you the albums, if you like. I'll bring them down to breakfast for you tomorrow.

'You remember the children's dining room? I wish we could restore it. So expensive to do that sort of thing now.'

He took a sip of the wine for her as she left. Then he got up from the table and went out through the stained-glass doors. He felt very strange. The food and wine were working.

On his way through the anteroom he rebuilt the children's dining room: the glossy floor, the cheerful red-checked table cloths, the shiny cutlery, the heavy white napkins stiff with starch, the chairs pushed in neatly beneath the tables, waiting. Then the rush of children into the room as the door was opened. Shrill voices, scraping clatter, chins above table edges, the grab for cutlery, fists shovelling at mouths, the ringing of spoons against plates, then an outburst in the corner and the spreading silence when he stood up aghast, his shoes shamefully splattered.

'It's the mountain air,' his mother said later in the room. 'He's a bit off colour.' She whipped out a thermometer and stuck it in his mouth. 'He's got a temp.'

His father looked on angrily. 'What's Ina been feeding him?'

TWENTY-THREE

Ina could not help herself. During their first week in Moresby she planted several trees in the bare grounds of the Papua Hotel. She walked up Paga Hill, discovered some healthy-looking tree seedlings and brought them back down. Then she extended the planting programme out into the sandy street. She went with Andrew on his tours in search of ideal land for a tobacco plantation, and collected plants from the Laloki valley and up towards Sogeri. She even bought some from planters there, mango seedlings mainly. She filled the saddlebags on the hired horses.

Coming back to town one time Andrew laughed. 'We're supposed to be planting, not damn well digging trees up.'

She was unperturbed. She put in mangoes all the way up Douglas Street from the hotel to the Government Secretary's Office. Then she proceeded with *Bombax, Sterculia* and wild nutmeg down Hunter Street to the Papua Club. By the time she reached that far—several weeks—she was the talking point of the town. She carried water to all of them by hand each evening, a task which became almost daunting as the line extended along Port Road past the Burns Philp main store. By then she had regular help in the form of the Director of Agriculture, Mr Whittaker, who lugged cans of water with her after work each day still dressed in his white office suit.

'This is all rather unofficial,' he grunted apologetically, his forehead awash with perspiration. 'His Excellency has not yet approved. I can't delegate a government work-party. Not yet.'

When a line of alternating *Garuga, Terminalia* and *Celtis* had turned the corner into steep Cuthbertson Street, the Director of Agriculture found her an unofficial four-wheeled trolley on which a large drum of water might be pulled along, which made the watering process much easier. And when she had planted her famous double row of pepper trees and *Nauclea* down Musgrave Street, even Lieutenant-governor Murray rode up to her one evening as she was dipping into the drum on the trolley, and made her acquaintance.

'Mrs Prideaux, isn't it?' He raised his felt hat, giving a glimpse of the high baldness of his head. She curtsied awkwardly as he went on, 'I wonder would you like some boys to help you in the evenings?'

She said she would indeed.

Hubert Murray mused for a moment, his hands twitching at the reins ever so slightly. 'I mean it as a permanent arrangement,' he said. 'Would you consider giving those self-same boys the opportunity of permanent employment by your acceptance of the curatorship of the botanic gardens?'

She looked up at him startled. 'Excuse me, Your Excellency,' she blurted, 'I didn't know there *was* a botanic gardens.'

'There isn't. That's the job, you see. To establish them. Do you accept?'

'I do,' she said, and felt foolish, for it sounded like a response at an altar.

The Curatorship of the Papuan Government Botanic Gardens was a long way from the greenhouse in the lane beside the Wagga Cash Store but Ina made the transition with ease. It was the kind of thing you had to do in Moresby in 1919. The place was like that. His Excellency, the Lieutenant-governor, Judge Hubert Murray rode up to you in the street dressed in khaki pants and blue shirt, lifted his incongruous grey city hat, and offered you a job. Just like that. Then he rode off. The white population of Moresby numbered only six hundred and thirty, and just one hundred and sixty-three of them were females. The small population of whites was responsible for almost an entire colony: its government, its education, its agriculture, its business, and its conversion to Christianity. Thus, an aloof, modest man of fifty-eight years who rode around the town on his horse

in the evenings, was in fact the governor, the biggest figure in
the colony's history (when it was later written) and the man
after whom they would name the colony's major road prior to
Independence: Sir Hubert Murray Drive. Similarly, a twenty-
four-year-old woman who had been in the tropics for only a few
weeks and who knew little more of plants than the everyday
hobbyist, was made Curator of the Botanic Gardens. And because, in addition, Lieutenant-governor Murray still stood at
six-foot-three (unbowed by his fifty-eight years) and had been
amateur heavy-weight boxing champion of Great Britain (as a
young man he had left Melbourne to study law at Oxford), he
had a soft spot for sport and gave thoughtful consideration to
Ina's impulsive proposal at their first official planning meeting:

'Well, sir. If we are to have a botanic gardens, why don't we
have a golf course as well? I could lay them out side by side.'

In the end—after an argument in the Legislative Council
over the propriety of using town land for a golf club when there
was already a cricket oval and tennis courts and a war memorial
park—it was the Lieutenant-governor's own decision that the
botanic gardens and the golf course should be created simul-
taneously and that their site would be the grounds of Government House itself, which were at that time well-grassed,
treeless, and used as a cow paddock.

As Ina established herself, so too did Andrew. He found a
stretch of land not far inland from Moresby which he thought
would suit tobacco. He planted ten acres initially, with smaller
plots of edible crops: familiar Australian things like blue pump-
kin, watermelon, tomatoes. He brought them to town for sale
each week, and though tough, wizened, or wormy, they sold
rapidly. Fresh civilised veges! The white women of Moresby
thought him a marvel. The stretch of land became known as
Prideaux's Estate, and his weekly drive to town along the rough
cart-track in the truck was a regular procession. Lining the way
the local villagers (especially the children) waited in the hope
that they might be given lifts. Since the truck moved so slowly
that even a toddler could keep up with it, the same crowd

repeated itself along the roadside—catching up, waiting, catching up again. It was two years before the next automobile came to Moresby, so for that brief period Prideaux's Chevrolet held the Papuan land speed record for automobiles at something less than walking pace.

It all sounds like fun, doesn't it Johnno? At times we believed it was.

Ina grew strong. She was even called 'tough' by some of the women in the town. It was jealousy speaking. They were suffering from tropical ennui. They disliked her for her trees right from the start. They disliked her for her foresight and bright ideas, and especially for her energy. The proper job of women in Moresby, they believed, was to be martyrs—to the climate, the isolation, the frailty of their sex and their husbands' arrant selfishness for ever bringing them there. Few among the female population had any sort of employment other than bossing their 'boys' around. Papuan servants did the child-minding, cooking, cleaning, washing and ironing. Tennis was played at the Tennis Club courts, swimming was done at the Aquatic Club enclosure, fancy dress balls were arranged at the Library Institute. Beyond that, social intercourse was mainly limited to complaints about the heat, the mosquitoes, the natives, the Lieutenant-governor, the absence of a town water supply, and the abominable length of time it took for any sort of news to arrive from Down South. The ladies of Moresby were exquisitely bored and stressed. Their greatest excitement occurred in the arguments that ensued when they threatened their husbands with leaving on the next boat South, which was never more than five weeks away. The Lieutenant-governor's wife had left him. She lived in style in Melbourne now. Why shouldn't they?

So, we weren't in paradise, Johnno. There were snakes in the kunai grass.

But Ina had employment and in the estimation of the town hers was a man-sized job. Hubert Murray told her he was not expecting results for a decade but she was determined to create appreciable shade in the Government House Gardens and in the streets of the town, in far less time than that.

'Water is all they need,' she told her line of Gulf men in the dry season, pointing them at yellowing *Spondias*. 'Drainage is all they need,' she said in the wet.

She learnt to speak Police Motu, the *lingua franca*, and out of necessity became fluent. If any of her boys had the audacity to complain or to ask needless directions about how to do something, she did not slap their faces with an open hand as was the accepted fashion in the colony, but instead said, 'Ask your dead grandfather. Get him to fix it up.' She always said it as if she were particular friends with that dead grandfather, and it always worked.

No, Johnno, I didn't have the time to be scared of my boys. I didn't have the leisure to make up stories about them looking at my legs or breathing hard when they were next to me. I left it to the silly women to make up those sorts of stories.

For the gardens she started with native species. Her budget was woefully small, there was no chance of a collection tour outside the colony. But amongst the files in the Director of Agriculture's office she found a leaflet describing the layout of Kew Gardens. She made use of it as her guide, enjoying the colonial absurdity of it. By matching as best she could Papuan species to the European species in the leaflet, she created a subtle replica of a corner of Kew Gardens adjacent to the verandas of Moresby's prefab Government House. It was Kew Gardens tropicalised and transformed, but strangely the same. This approach to the planting of the gardens caused considerable controversy, especially since she gave it plenty of publicity in her weekly gardening article in the *Papuan Times*. She found that her gardens touched at the heart of colonial ideologies. Letters began appearing in the paper signed by anonymous townspeople who called themselves 'Hiri', 'Laurabada', and the like. They ridiculed her for planting native species at all. They wanted 'exotic' trees like the oak and the ash. One correspondent wrote, 'If Moresby is truly to establish itself as a civilised town, if the colony is ever properly to be tamed by Australians, then we must clear the country entirely, burn what we can't sell, and establish paying industries.' That one signed himself 'Botanical Bungles'.

One gentler critic, the Lieutenant-governor himself, wondered privately in her presence whether the Kew plan was entirely necessary. 'It seems to have drawn the wrong sort of attention,' he said.

But she persisted. 'Good heavens, there has to be *some* nonsensical order,' she told him. 'The whole colony is a botanic gardens otherwise.'

You see, Johnno? I loved the country. I never took the 'black peril' seriously. And worse than that, I never took the women of Moresby seriously. If I lay awake at night full of fearful imaginings under my hot mosquito net it was Louise and Cliffie I thought about—how safe they were, how loved. I didn't lie there imagining black shadows climbing the veranda stairs, slipping through the french doors.

Where she saw barrenness she struck. Some of her main weapons were ferns and orchids. Several thatched shelters were built near the Government House stables and she began a propagation programme. Any dull government office or bare front veranda became her target. The unadorned verandas of Government House (where the Legislative Council met) were the first to sprout elkhorns and staghorns. His abstemious Excellency received quite a shock on the first morning when he came out for a gentle round with the punching-bag which hung at the far end of the veranda and found a jungle of waving *Platycerium bifurcatum* greeting him. Then this jungle spread to the town. Letters handed across the counter at the post office were almost intercepted by a huge wall-hung *Arachnanthe*. The Commissioner of Native Affairs sweated and cursed between two very large *Rhododendrons* which soon took over his office. And one woman at the Betel Social Club rooms was assaulted during a tea party by a burgeoning vine known as the D'Albertis Creeper.

So plants became political in Moresby, and as a policy often becomes identified with a politician, so plants became identified with Ina. No one in the town could look at the spreading shade from a young vigorous *Delonix* without thinking of Ina Prideaux. Few couples could sit on their verandas without the company of an aggressive *Platycerium bifurcatum* which owed its very conception to Ina. The biggest of them all, Ina had on her own veranda. Some women, out of spite, sent their houseboys out to tear off flowers and branches from the street trees to leave them denuded and unsightly. Ina had Sir Hubert pass an ordinance to deal with tree vandals.

I should have seen it coming then, shouldn't I, Johnno?

Ina's influence spread among the Papuans too. Jobs on her labour line were greatly prized. The Papuan men enjoyed working with the white woman who got her hands dirty beside them.

'Look at that mulchy soil,' she would yell at them. 'It's good enough to eat.'

And when one of them pretended to lift it to his mouth she would laugh.

She amazed the Papuans. She was the only white woman in Moresby who was human. By comparison the rest of them seemed to be made of stone. But she was a tyrant at times too. If the dead grandfather of one of her men simply was not showing him how to do a job properly, she would barge in, grab the Papuan's hands, and forcefully direct them in the correct method to be used. For practically all who received this treatment it was the first time they had touched a white woman, felt her skin or the bones beneath her gardening gloves.

The first attack occurred in 1924, Johnno. There was another a year later. Then two more. White women were the victims. 'The jungle has entered the town,' I heard people say. Moresby began to get very frightened. Women were sleeping with guns under their pillows. Sir Hubert passed curfew laws to keep the Papuans away from the whites at night. A special group of constables patrolled the streets after dark. A system of passes for Papuans was introduced. There was talk of building a tall wire fence around the town. And one pseudonymous resident in the letters column ('Sinabada' she signed herself) even said that Governor Murray was to blame because he had encouraged the likes of me to degrade the authority of the white woman in the colony.

Once the horticulture was firmly established, Ina turned her thoughts to the golf course. For several months she built up a picture in her mind of the perfect four holes. She tailored the vision precisely to suit the moderately steep Government House grounds. She imagined so vividly that she knew where every tree, every rise, every tee and trap would be. She played them over and over for months in her head, foreseeing shots of every kind and distance, in an attempt to know exactly how it would turn out in reality. Only when she was certain of the plan did she get the men to start digging the bunkers and transferring the dug earth to raise the tees and greens. The work went well, but it was more than a year before the abbreviated course was playable. She had at times an army of men working on it. She and the dead grandfathers had to order them about as stridently as sergeant-majors. In the end she created a marvellous links overlooking the Moresby harbour and Hanuabada village: a par three, a par five, and two par fours. They had coarse, rather bumpy greens, trimmed kunai fairways and crushed coral bunkers. She played the course several times herself before the official opening and found it most challenging. She had not realised in conceiving it that it would reflect her own personality, but she had the feeling when she played that she was up against herself, face-to-face with her own difficulties. It was short, steep and unforgiving—but you could beat it, there was that satisfaction available. When it opened to the public the men criticised it for being 'a woman's course', but the women said it was too hard.

The attacks increased. A woman woke to find her houseboy lying on top of her. A policeboy assaulted a four-year-old girl...

During this period of the late 'twenties Moresby changed from a complacent trading port to a nervy, complex town. A small but noisy 'smart set' did the Charleston in the new Turf Club and turned out in mixed groups on the golf course. Several fast cars were imported and planters' sons drove them down the lines of coconut palms. Andrew bought one, an Australian Six, and managed a spectacular crash into the sea at Koki when his brakes failed on the Badili Hill. The talkies arrived in the cinema and whites and blacks (at segregated screenings) were astonished by the verisimilitude produced on the canvas screen. But they soon became sophisticated, even blasé, and by the time Errol Flynn began appearing in the early 'thirties most of

Port Moresby's movie-goers coolly accepted that one of the town's legendary drunken scoundrels had become a big star.

At one point in the expansion of his tobacco empire Andrew bought the plantation Flynn had attempted to start, up towards Sogeri. Ina and Andrew spent weekends on that beautiful property beside the Laloki River in a house built and abandoned by Flynn. Ina found, to her annoyance, that the trunks of many of the large trees there had been mutilated by deep etchings. Hearts, arrows, initials, and more elaborate erotic signs, had been carved by a heavy, competent hand. It was Andrew who deduced the significance of the graffiti: Errol had designated particular trees for the seduction of particular Papuan women, or that is what he wished people to think. Sir Hubert stayed there with Ina and Andrew on several occasions, using the place as a staging point on his way to Kokoda. In spite of his reputation as a stick-in-the-Papuan-mud, Sir Hubert often laughed at Flynn's having carved himself into Papuan history.

'Come up and see my etchings sometime,' Sir Hubert would quip, then try to translate that into Motuan, as he and Ina strolled by the fast brown river.

Sir Hubert could not help his private fondness for Flynn, it seemed. He had been a boxer too, of course. But in his public role Sir Hubert showed no such flippancy over mixed-race sexual matters. In the wake of the spate of sexual attacks by Papuan men on white women Sir Hubert had authored the most draconian piece of criminal legislation ever seen in the British Empire: the White Women's Protection Ordinance. It decreed the death penalty for any Papuan who even attempted to rape a white female.

The first Papuan was hung in 1927, Johnno. It was a shocking affair. He was found in the hallway of a house where a white woman was sleeping. That was his crime: being there. Even the Australian press thought the punishment was shocking. And there were several more hangings. They were crimes against the Papuan nation, and crimes against justice itself.

Ina's strained belief in the innocence of golf and gardens and weekly newspaper columns and strolls with the Governor was ended completely in 1932. Some women in the town—wives of the businessmen and planters who were members of the Citizens' Committee and the Papua Club—made up stories about her and Sir Hubert. Unpleasant, snide stories. Because their husbands hated Sir Hubert's Native Labour policy, his Native Lands policy, his Native Everything policy. They saw the closeness between Ina and the Governor and took the political advantage. But they also saw Ina with her hands in the same dirt as her labour line boys and embroidered their suspicions into outrageous, gross stories. Because Andrew Prideaux's tobacco plantations were doing better than their husbands' copra plantations and because he was talking about a cigarette-making factory in Port Moresby which would be the first major manufacturing venture in the colony, the Moresby wives told their husbands to tell their stories to Prideaux. And that made things difficult for Ina and Andrew because he loved her enough to be jealous just at the suggestion, and she loved him enough to be deeply hurt by his giving credence.

All of this led in 1932 to a famous incident which was not reported in the *Papuan Times* (it did not have to be, everyone knew of it) where thirty-eight-year-old Andrew ungallantly swung a punch at seventy-year-old Sir Hubert on the veranda of Government House one night after a long and involved argument. A split-second after the impotent swing, Andrew was sent flat on his back by a fist which he never saw coming and which landed square on his chin.

Having left Government House to give his jaw and his pride a great deal of tender care in the form of gin-slings at the Papua Club, Andrew staggered home down Stanley Parade and, after a difficult mounting of the tall wooden stairs to the front door of his house, discovered a Gulf Papuan standing on the veranda in the dark beneath Ina's monstrous staghorn beside the french doors which, had they been open, would have given direct access to Ina and Andrew's bedroom.

Andrew grabbed the man and wrestled with him across the veranda and down the stairs into the garden. Angered by his earlier defeat that evening, Andrew was tenacious. He rolled with the black body in the garden, cleaving to its heat and slipperiness. The Gulf man did not get away. The constables of the town patrol, hearing the neighbours shouting, ran down the street to make the arrest. Ina came out onto the veranda and in her innocence looked down on the man held in the garden.

'Vaimuru!' she called with relief, knowing he was innocent. 'You can let him go. I shall take responsibility for him.'

The constables ignored her. They led the man away into the darkness, and Andrew went with them.

Ina was shocked. She did not sleep. She stood at the french doors waiting for Andrew's return. She watched the harbour gently emerge from darkness, like a bromide in a photographic tank. She saw it fill with the naked softness of dawn light. Then Andrew came sheepishly up the stairs and pushed through the doors.

'What happened?' she asked, her voice urgent with concern. 'Did he get home all right?'

'They're holding him. He's been charged.'

'What charge? You laid a charge?'

'I only laid a complaint.'

'Well, you have to withdraw it.'

'It's all out of my hands. I hardly know what happened. It had barely anything to do with me.'

'You raised the alarm. You shouted for the constables.'

'Of course I did. To help me arrest the fellow.'

'The fellow? It was Vaimuru.'

'I couldn't let him get away.'

She turned from him. Through the doorway the harbour was now clear and blue. Off Hanuabada, the crab's-claw sail was rising on a huge *lakatoi*. Andrew left the bed where he had been sitting and came up behind her. He put his arms around her but she stayed tightly drawn against him.

'I'm sorry, love,' he said. 'I was drunk and hurt and angry.'

'You shouldn't have yelled for the constables.'

'But he was right outside the door.'

'Why didn't you ask him what he was doing?'

'God Almighty, Ina. I saw a native right outside the bedroom. Was I supposed to politely ask him his intentions? Do you think he would have told the truth?'

'Well, you could have asked me. I was asleep in here. You could have woken me. Or did you suppose that was equally pointless?'

He hugged her, but she stayed cold. 'I don't know what I supposed at the time, love. I panicked. I saw an invader...'

She twisted from his embrace. 'Well, he hadn't invaded *me*.'

She dressed and left the house. She walked the harbour road to Government House. On her left the harbour waters crept and dallied among the mangrove roots. On her right the golf course stretched dry and deserted in the morning sun. She climbed the shady drive to Government House and mounted the stairs.

Sir Hubert was at breakfast on the veranda. Amongst the official files piled on the table there was little room for his teapot and plates of pawpaw and toast.

It came as a shock to her to realise that he was not pleased to see her. He lowered his eyes as she came up the steps. He put down the slice of lime he had been squeezing over the wedge of pawpaw, and brought his napkin fastidiously to his moustache. She ignored his reserved manner. She clumped along the veranda towards him.

'He didn't do anything,' she said. 'He must be released.'

'I can't do that.' He put the napkin down on a file on the table. 'He has been charged under the law.'

'You can tell them to drop the charge.'

'The law is not like that, my dear.'

She noticed the lack of warmth in the 'my dear'.

'But you *wrote* the law. You know what's wrong with it.'

'I know I drew it up. And I abhor every word in it.'

'Why can't you change it then?'

'Because it is for the natives' own good.'

'For the *innocent* natives' own good?'

'You are a white woman, my dear. Your safety must be sacrosanct.'

'But my safety was never threatened.'

'You don't know that. The law will decide.'

'But you could change the law. You wrote it.'

'My dear. The law is not mine to change. It was an enact-
ment of the Legislative Council.'

'The six of you fellows sitting here on the veranda? At this
table? Ralph Whittaker, Charles Mont—'

'Now you are being obtuse. The law isn't like that. It's
greater than that.'

He sat in silence for a moment, his hand on the edge of the
table, his eyes on his breakfast. He would not look up at her.

'Is the law greater than innocence?' she asked.

'Yes. It is greater than innocence and guilt, both.'

She refused to turn from the table until he looked at her, and
when he did at last, she saw the naked vulnerability in his eyes,
and worse than that, Johnno, the unspoken accusation.

She turned and fled down the fairways towards the road.

TWENTY-FOUR

By the end of his first year (it was 1972) John was convinced that life in Moresby suited him perfectly. Goffett's prediction about big fish in a small pool was correct: it was easy to make a mark as a town planner in a stone-age country hellbent on modernisation. In his social life too John was finding satisfaction. A regular round of weekend parties in glorious tropical settings (the bays, the islands, the mountains around the town) introduced him to the tight-knit community of public servants, journalists and teachers who had come to Moresby in circumstances similar to his own.

He loved being in the air and sunshine of Moresby. Their zest and clarity quickened him. Then in the wet season he loved the madness of the sudden downpours—rain which fell in exuberant warm curtains and could be happily walked through. It drenched then dried off rapidly with the returning sun. And after the rain he loved the rich leafy odours, the wild celery fragrance of the kunai grass beside the red dirt roads, the pig grease and woodfire smells emanating from rambling shacks in the local suburbs and settlements.

Moresby became his stage. He discovered a part to play which matched his sense of self. He delighted in the weekend group of friends who drank and swam and idled together, but who cared for each other as family. On weekdays he threw himself into his work where Goffett gave him a free hand in several major projects. To celebrate his new-found confidence he conceived the idea of affecting a bow tie at official functions (not the whirring version which came a little later), feeling certain that he was the only man in the entire tropics who was mad enough to wear a bow tie, making that his trade mark.

In his work he found amusement and challenge in the ironies of white men planning towns for a ten-thousand-year-old culture. He and Goffett had the task of assessing the social impact of the government's proposed showpiece—a new town called Waigani to be built on grasslands on the outskirts of Moresby in time for Independence. It would feature at its centre a Parliament House shaped like an upturned boat, an Australian Embassy taller than every other building, a Prime Ministerial office block resembling a giant pineapple wearing a plastic hat, and a six-lane super highway, to be called Independence Drive, which would run for a kilometre and stop abruptly. The proposed town was all for show. It was meant to make the statement: 'Look how far Papua New Guinea has come to gain Independence'. But as John perceived, it said something quite different. It showed the country's new *dependence* on the twentieth century, on international politics and macroeconomics, on aid and pressures from outside, on concrete and plastic.

John devoted himself to the Waigani plan because he saw it was also very Papua New Guinean. It was a mad, tinsel-wreathed dance of buildings. It was bombast in a new architectural language. It was the new elite's big-time squatter settlement showing off muscles of steel.

On a typical weekend John drove down to Bugandi Bay for a party on a converted twin-hulled canoe. There were seven men present. They motored out across the broad reef-mottled bay, past Tatana Island, to the farthest reaches of the harbour where the mountains swept up from inlets, their grass-covered slopes rippling like velvet in the seasonal breeze. The men took off their clothes and swam in the pearly water among corals and rainbow-coloured fish.

On the deck, sunbathing and drinking, the men delighted in talk about Moresby—how shocking, how primitive, how logical a town it was. The flies on the unrefrigerated wallaby carcasses at Koki market, and the village couple who tried to sell a smoked baby there before the authorities confiscated it; the dangers of 'payback' reprisals if a European driver knocked down a local pedestrian, and how the Papua New Guineans ranked the car a deadlier weapon than the spear and did not subscribe to the notion that every time a car ran into something it was an accident; the story which had appeared in the papers during the week of a man who had fallen gravely ill after tearing up a Bible for a dare and, having been rushed to hospital by ambulance, turned into a python in the hospital bed, as reported by visiting relatives; the arrest of the self-styled Kung Fu Man who had attacked the Burns Philp Freezer windows with his bare hands in front of a crowd and lifted his bleeding palms to take the applause.

Lying back in a plastic chair on the boat deck with alcohol in his head and the sun in the recesses of his body, John felt the stories of Moresby enter his brain like a stirring drug. Port Moresby was *his* village, he was certain. He felt comfortably at home. And when two of the friends floated off to the foredeck to enjoy sex in the drumming sunshine the talk did not miss a beat.

At the beginning of his second year John was given an assistant. His name was Francis Tapukai. He was a graduate from the university, and a Tolai. He was brilliant, shifty, handsome. During work hours he was gentle and charming. Outside work hours he was a monstrous drinker and betelnut addict. He arrived late in the office every morning with the reddest blood-shot eyes John ever saw. He was erratic in his work, but his brilliance far outweighed his faults. His understanding of the impact of modern pressures on Papua New Guineans, his articulation of those pressures, and his suggestions for acceptable solutions, formed the basis for most of the plans that John's office produced prior to Independence Day. There was no doubt that Francis Tapukai had a bright future: he took to town planning like a crocodile to water. Yet his village orientation did not seem to waver.

During Francis' first week in the office, while the two were poring over plans together, John asked him about the Tolai *warbat*.

Francis smiled coyly. 'You know about *warbat*, John?'

'I've heard of it.'

The *warbat* was one of the titillating topics John's friends discussed. When a Tolai man wanted a particular woman to fall in love with him he engaged the services of a *warbat* singer. By chanting *warbat* love charms the singer would draw the chosen woman from the hut where she slept and lead her, by song, to the lover waiting in the jungle.

'It's top secret magic, John.'

'Tell me about it then.'

Francis looked down at the plan spread out on the table in front of them. It was, of all things, the design for a public convenience to be placed near Independence Drive. Francis ran his finger along the lines of the plan. 'Shouldn't we be discussing Waigani?'

John shook his head. 'I want to know about *warbat.*'

'I have some songs on tape. Would you like to hear them?'

John went to Francis' place that night. Francis lived in Boroko, another Moresby suburb, in a small flat provided by the government. It was the first time John had been in a Papua New Guinean's home. He felt awkward. The flat was bare-walled, mattress-strewn, lit by naked bulbs. It smelt of sweat and sleep. But Francis was a capable, if uncomplicated, host. He pulled out beers from the fridge (proud of their coldness) and switched on the small Japanese cassette player. The *warbat* singing came into the room.

'Tolai women are scared of it,' Francis laughed. 'Even those who go to the university.'

John had to admit immediately that there was something powerful about the songs, something hypnotic even to a sceptical European.

'Do they work on white women?' he asked.

Francis smiled coyly again. 'Haven't you heard about my reputation?' He laughed with his face tilted downwards.

The singing was by marvellous male voices, falsetto and gravelly at once, punctuated by a bamboo xylophone. The song seemed to come in pulsating waves. John drank beer and closed his eyes. He felt the singing vibrate in his chest and spine. Was it the earth singing? It seemed like voices coming from wood, from leaves, from soil and falling water. He could hear the singers' breathing, could feel the closeness of them, of the song's intimacy, coming from inside himself now; yet, at the same time, the song shifted, built and vanished, like faraway cloud churning. Immobile in his chair, he felt he travelled through transparent membranes, one vista opening upon another. As the singing paused and surged he went with it, dreading and loving it, falling and climbing with an irresistible momentum, tumbling into the gulfs of the song, soaring up the mountainsides of the song.

The music stopped. 'I'm stoned,' John said, opening his eyes.

Francis sat in the chair opposite with his head thrown back and his smooth neck exposed. His Adam's apple was rising and falling gently. '*Liu liu liu,*' he sang, echoing the song.

After a few more beers and much laughter, John drove home through the squatter settlement beyond Boroko and Badili. He stopped the car at no place in particular and got out simply to experience the rich night air, the tropic sky rattling with stars, the overhanging trees with their pendant darknesses, the warmth rising from ditches beside the roadway, and the dark house yards screened by banana plants out of which came low laughter or talk or arguments, all carried on in darkness except for the pink glow of embers and the occasional garish pressure lamp. He breathed in the wood smoke, the tang of tropical blossoms, the exhalations of humid earth. Willingly, he opened his consciousness to the shadows and murmurs and dark fragrances surrounding him, and felt a subtle rearrangement inside, as if the suburbs of his soul were being invaded and taken over by new inhabitants.

The next Saturday John invited Francis to go with him to the swimming pool. It was a calculated move, he knew, and he did not wish to examine his motives too closely. He fully expected that Francis would decline, but after hesitating for a moment, as if he had another engagement which he was deciding to cancel, Francis said he would like to go.

It was the Saturday after a pay-day Friday. On the verges of

111

Sir Hubert Murray Drive lay the occasional car wreck, as was normal following the pay-night spree. Drunkenness was endemic in Moresby on a fortnightly basis. John paid for Francis' admission into the pool and they found a patch of grass down by the cyclone wire fence, away from the European families and the talkative locals. Francis did not bring a towel. Expecting this, John had brought two of them which he spread out on the grass.

John tried not to look too directly at Francis' body as he stripped down to a pair of Speedo swimming trunks. During the week John had taken note whenever Francis hinted at his sexual prowess among women. John had no expectations and no definite evidence regarding Francis' preferences, but he did have an instinct. His radar was working. In any case, he could not resist the sight of a taut, handsome body under any circumstances. Perhaps fortunately, a pair of drunken highlanders arrived and clung to the outside of the wire fence to watch the antics of those who could afford admission to the pool. Their shirts were undone, their trousers awry. They provided a distraction.

'A big night on the road last night,' John commented awkwardly.

Francis lay down on the towel. 'Yes, plenty of parties. Drunkenness is a sacred state here.'

John knew that was true. Some parties were held in the middle of main roads, with the cartons of stubbies piled up on the double white lines. Drivers had to manoeuvre around the seated drinkers until the police came to remove them.

'You get sent to gaol for it in Australia.'

Francis frowned. 'Oh, drunkenness is your best excuse for anything here. If you roll your car off the road because you are drunk, well, that is your defence, isn't it? You were drunk, so it happened. You should not be punished again by being sent to gaol.'

John snorted. 'You don't subscribe to that, do you?'

'It is the unofficial view, I think.'

The two drunks still clung happily to the fence. John was reminded of the zoo; but was disturbed by the knowledge that he was on the enclosed side of the cage fence. The drunks grinned, and he smiled back at them. One of them, he noticed, wore a grubby T-shirt which had printed on it: 'I am Independent. I don't need to drink.'

'Oh, and another thing, John. Never laugh at someone who is drunk. A drunk man cannot help the way he looks.' Then Francis burst into a fit of high-pitched laughter. 'I am only pulling your leg, mate,' he spluttered.

John felt a strange vulnerability to Francis. There was something about the black man that struck at him deep down. He felt a stirring desperation to please Francis, to 'pleasure' him was perhaps the word. He wanted to impress him, and somehow to support him.

They swam languidly together in the pool, but found the splashing and screeching of the surrounding children a nuisance. They hauled themselves out and sat for a while in the sun on the pool's edge. John saw the suave shape of Francis' penis moulded in his wet swimmers and felt a sort of drunkenness pass through him.

When they went back to their towels the clinging highlanders had gone.

After just a month of working side by side with Francis Tapukai, John knew that his developing inverted racism had become focused towards the Tolai. He was turning into a Tolai culture buff, and a Gazelle Peninsula supporter. The Mataungans could do no wrong. Francis Tapukai could do no wrong. When Francis failed to present his work on time, John finished it for him. When Francis lied about goofing off in work time, John provided the alibis. When stories were told about Francis' affairs with white women, John was jealous.

During their first weeks of friendship Francis introduced John to the Boroko Hotel beer garden. The place was notorious for its brawls which the hotel management had to clear with high-pressure hoses. John got a kick out of drinking there. His Australian colleagues called it the Snake Pit. They told him stories about highlanders dragging broken stubbie bottles through the soft white throats of expatriates who entered there.

113

But John discovered such stories to be nonsense. Certainly it was a black men's enclave, but he went there regularly with Francis and survived. And he knew why. He did not emanate prejudice and hatred. Prejudice was like sweat, he thought. You could smell it.

John and Francis were there together one evening, drinking at a concrete table under the rubber trees. Francis was moody, a little uncommunicative, as was common. John happened to look up and saw three brawny Australians come out of the pub lounge and into the beer garden. These men *did* stink of prejudice. The babble of the fifty or so Papua New Guineans drinking on the concrete seats dried up immediately. The three big whites came down the aisle between the concrete tables in an aggressive phalanx. John innocently wondered whether these fellows were newcomers in Moresby. He speculated as to whether they could be drivers of the giant bulldozers on the Bougainville Copper Project. Meanwhile, the three monsters were coming straight towards John and Francis' table. Before John properly knew what had happened, one of the three had sent his fist flying into Francis' face, knocking him sprawling on the concrete paving. The other two delivered full-blooded kicks to Francis' kidneys and head via steel-toed work boots. Then they walked out.

There was no eruption in the Snake Pit. The servery gates were not hurriedly rolled down, nor were the fire hoses manned by the hotel staff, as usually happened at the first hint of a brawl. Instead, Francis lay bleeding from the nose on the concrete while a crowd of black faces stared at him, immobile.

John bent down and tried to lift him under the shoulders. 'Jesus, Francis. Let's go.'

Francis allowed himself to be hauled to his feet. Then he sat again, shakily, at the table.

'I'll bring the car around to the gate.'

Francis shook his head. 'Stay and drink, *poro*.' He was forcing a laugh, holding his hands over his hurt face.

John protested, but it was no use. He went to the servery for more beer. *Perhaps he has to show his countrymen that he is a man.*

Damned Tolai pride. John brought the open bottles back to the table. Francis edged one towards his bleeding mouth.

'I met her in the bar last night.' Francis spoke softly. 'I just met her and she asked me to come to the room upstairs. I couldn't help it.'

'Who, Francis? Who are you talking about?'

'That fellow's wife. The one who hit me.'

'Jesus Christ. You must be mad.'

Francis smiled. Freeman saw the blood and beer froth swimming over his teeth.

'European women fall in love with me like that,' Francis said.

They drank until the beer garden closed. Then John insisted on taking Francis back home with him. As they drove past the Burns Philp supermarket they heard the cascading shatter of plate glass. Ahead of them highlanders spilt across the road. They charged about, picking up the rocks lining the trampled garden beds in the park opposite, using them to smash the windows of the Chinese shop fronts along Tabari Place.

'It's starting,' Francis said.

He was slumped in the bucket seat beside John, his head against the side window. He didn't turn to look as John threaded the car through the wild movement of men.

'What's starting?'

The car received several thumps along its side. A rock came through the back window on John's side, shattering the glass which spilt into the back seat.

'Independence is starting.'

They drove out of Boroko along Sir Hubert Murray Drive, over the hill and down into Badili. The sound of the riot reverberated behind them. *There are currents beneath the surface which I am disqualified from seeing.* John's thinking was a maze of vulnerabilities, but at the centre of it was something hard and selfish—an inexorable lust. He drove home quickly and parked the car right outside his front steps.

In the bathroom John sponged dried blood from Francis' face. Francis took off his shirt. He twisted to look in the mirror at the bruises from the kicking in his side and back. In the quavering fluorescent light John could see the swelling under the shinier patches of dark skin. Francis was disarmingly cheerful about the sight of his own injuries. He admired them for a time. Then he turned to John and laughed. 'I need a hot shower for the bruises.' He stripped the rest of his clothes off.

An exhibition. A seduction. A sudden view in a disturbing mirror.

Through the bathroom louvres the haunting sound of the riot pulsed across the hill from Boroko.

Francis took John's soap, shampoo, and toothbrush into the shower recess and turned the hot water to full blast without drawing the curtain. John went and sat in the lounge room, excited, hearing the riot far off, a wavering blur of sound in the night and, close by, through the walls, heard Francis singing a pained-sounding Tolai song, brushing his teeth at the same time.

It is one of those songs. The warbat. Liu liu liu.

When Francis came into the lounge room, dripping, laughing, saying, 'Hey, John. Will you go and bring me a towel?' John was gone, plummeting, unsavable. Under the clattering fan in the dark bedroom they did what they could not possibly avoid doing, with the riotous night receding outside open louvre windows.

In the early hours of the morning John drove Francis to his flat. The streets were still. It seemed as if the riot had dispersed, although a police wagon sped by them at one intersection and vanished into the night.

Turning into Francis' street they heard a thumping. It grew louder as they neared his place.

'The stewardesses,' Francis laughed. 'They have parties every night. Even a riot cannot stop them.'

Parking in Francis' drive John could hear clearly the words of the amplified music (the Rolling Stones singing 'Brown Sugar') and the punctuating rumpus of party abandon.

'The Air Niugini dormitory,' Francis explained.

Through the intervening cyclone wire fence John could see a riot of floral-coloured lap-laps, of strewn brown bodies and beer bottles under an outdoor spotlight. He had to admit there was an amusing, tawdry glamour about it all. These crazy drunks kept the aeroplanes flying! A bottle sailed through the air and smashed against a wall.

'Do they keep you awake?' John asked.

'Oh, no. Not really.'

'Do you ever go and join them?'

'Of course not. They are not the kind of women I am interested in. I think they prefer white men.'

Standing in the dark garden beside the tall wire fence, John felt a sudden urge to reassert his claim on territory. Another bottle soared and plummeted beyond the spotlight and John turned and caressed Francis through his shorts.

'You want to fuck again, mate?'

The Rolling Stones came to the end of the song. Some drunken hand in the night skidded the needle back to the start and the record began all over again.

'Brown sugar...'

TWENTY-FIVE

John could not eat breakfast. He had had a bad night, and he knew the sips of chardonnay were the catalyst. He wondered whether the agony was comparable to that of a gut full of shrapnel in Vietnam. He supposed it was. *My private Vietnam. All the way with being gay. Ha.*

He remembered telling Francis about the fist-fucking on stage at the Dungeon, off Oxford Street in Sydney. That's where he had misspent too many annual leave periods. Ten years in a row he flew to Sydney from Port Moresby. Flew in like the jet-setting boys from California. Ah, California boys, bronzed and oiled and shorn smooth. They stopped going to Vietnam and came to Sydney. 'Nobody told us what Vietnam would be like. No, sir. Nobody told us we would die.' He had groped with them at the Dungeon, had danced at parties. *And nobody told them love was more dangerous than war.* Ah, California boys, dancing to their deaths. *Funny. Francis never believed my stories about fist-fucking at the Dungeon. Yet Francis believed in Taxi Number 33.* Kaposi's sarcoma. It sounded like a Tolai dance step. Or at least a Tolai name. *Francis Kaposi Sakoma Tapukai.* Oh, Jesus.

Sitting in the wastes of the Hydro Majestic dining room among the museum pieces with bare toast and little air-tight packets of butter and Vegemite and marmalade staring up at him, John tried to avoid imagining his own bowels. Inside, in the dark there, those fucking nodules were swelling and swelling. Like the tiny bodies of dead boys in dark car boots.

Bloating up. Dark brown secrets which his body hadn't been game to show to the world. One of his friends in Sydney had had the blotches on the outside, on his legs and chest, but John had got them on the secret skin of his gut.

No, he couldn't eat anything, could barely look at food, but he buttered his toast and cut it into pieces and pushed it around so that it looked partly eaten. He poured half a cup of tea so that it looked half drunk. He watched Mrs West dishing out bacon and eggs and kippers and hash browns and God knows what else at the servery. She didn't look across at him. He thought maybe she had forgotten her promise of last night. He looked around at the five couples in the dining room. They were the same five couples who had sat down to dinner the previous night. They were dressed up, apparently ready to check out after breakfast. Perhaps no one stayed more than one night in the Hydro these days? When he had come here as a kid with his parents they had always stayed at least a week.

The dining room began to empty. An employee brought in a stepladder and began hanging Christmas decorations from the ceiling. It was July. Even the seasons were upside-down at the Hydro. 'We've got a Yuletide celebration this weekend,' the workman told him. 'We usually do it this time of year. Attracts a lot of guests. Log fires and so on. Quite often it snows on cue.' Winter in Australia. As far from Christmas as you could get.

Mrs West had not forgotten. Now that the dining room was, apart from John, empty of guests, she carried three albums over to his table. From the design of their covers it appeared that they had been put together in the 'fifties, but most of the photographs were much older than that. He spent an hour looking through them. He skipped over the Hydro's hydropathic spa years: the turn-of-the-century plumbing had its fascination, but he was in no mood to dwell on an era of sick people desperate to be well, and of spartan, cell-like rooms; but he did notice, in quickly turning the pages, how there was no photograph of a sufferer fallen down or being taken away in the back of an ambulance. *I don't want to think about it.* Apart from the bizarre shots of sunken-eyed patients having hoses played on their chests and buttocks, the photographs showed the hydropathic clinic guests as a remarkably healthy lot all having a marvellous time.

He moved on to the war years and the 'twenties and 'thirties. The wild waltzing in the hotel's casino, the chorus girls, the billiard tables, the masked balls. All gone these days, except for the Kiplingesque friezes on the casino walls, discoloured but still vaguely challenging.

John looked for Ina. *It's her face I want to see.* Absurdly optimistic, he sought for her among the crowds of anonymous snow-ball throwers in the winter scenes, and among the sun bathers in the glens in the summers. Perhaps his optimism was not entirely misplaced. She *had* lived there for eight years until the American servicemen came, and for another fourteen years after they had left. She must have been practically an institution in the hotel. He studied the faces in the soft-grained images. Which was she? Which of those smiling revellers was his grandmother? There was no white circle identifying her face in a large group with the caption: INA STOCKS (CIRCLED).

He went slowly through the American years too. One of those bed-ridden, cigarette-smoking servicemen was his father. Not an American, but in the American forces just the same, seconded to the American Navy as a harbour pilot. He searched the faces. At first none of them bore any family resemblance. But as his eyes tired they all began to look the same, and all like his father. Gaunt-faced, thinned by war. Yet smiling. Perhaps they weren't sick or wounded. Perhaps they were faking it. All Yossarians. Or perhaps they were like himself, dying from the inside.

He kept going to the 'fifties, to surreal scenes of Holdens in the hotel drive covered in winter snow, to tableau-like shots taken in summer of family picnics on the cliff top with the plastic picnic plates and the anodised picnic drinking cups and the portable barbecues. 'Waltzing Matildas' those three-legged barbecues were called. Aussie lifestyle. *Aussie deathstyle.* But Ina wasn't there. His parents weren't there. He was looking for himself in those photos too, but he found nothing. His family wasn't part of the official photographic history of the Hydro Majestic. *But we were there. We were in that crowd. I was one of those crew-cut boys in knee-length shorts.* He felt his own boy-ghost trying to push in at the margins of the photographs. *I was there. The pictures don't show it. But I was there. With Ina. With Ina telling me about black boys being hung.* He tried to remember if he had carved his own initials on a rock anywhere along the cliff edge in good Aussie-kid style. He was sure he had not. He wasn't that sort of boy.

He carried the albums back to Mrs West's office. She sat behind a desk, puffing on a cigarette. 'What did you think of those?' she asked through the smoke.

'Wonderful.'

'There are some coloured ones. They're away at the framers. I'm going to hang them in the new lounge when it's finished. I'm sorry you can't see them now. But I like the old black and whites. They're the right colour for history, don't you think?'

Even as he laughed politely his thinking sparred with the idea. National history might be in black and white but personal history was in the washed-out colours of 8 mm Kodachrome . . . his mother in blurry red shorts descending the sunlight-dashed stairs carrying a tray with a bottle of beer for his father . . . Always for his father.

Silent home movies. The silence they always held over me.

'What about Ina Stocks? Did you find anything on her?'

Mrs West encircled her beehive with smoke. 'She's easy to find in the register. She used to arrange the golf parties at Blackheath. We never had our own golf course. The balls would all be going over the cliff, I suppose. It's bad enough with the tennis courts, even though the fences are eighteen feet high.'

John could not help imagining it. A tee on the cliff top, the green a thousand feet below in the gorge. What a hole! To drive straight out into the vertiginous gulf. To watch the ball lift and soar, then level out, hang as if suspended on a string scorning gravity, with the great maw of the gorge waiting. Then the plummet.

'But what about Ina's daily life here? She was quite an attraction in the hotel, wasn't she? A famous columnist and golfer?'

'There are newspaper clippings, and some correspondence . . .'

'Yes?'

'She was rather an eccentric . . .'

'Yes?'

'She ended up embarrassing the hotel.'

'By going mad?'

'By striking a golf ball all down the corridors. She injured several guests.' Mrs West put another cigarette to her lipstick-red lips and lit it. 'One woman had to have stitches. Hotels don't appreciate that sort of publicity.'

John could not think of anything to say. He supposed his parents had had to pay compensation but he had never heard mention of it. He knew of Ina's madness, but had not realised anyone had been hurt. And oddly, Mrs West seemed to take it personally, as if the ball from Ina's swinging iron shot had been driven into the side of her own head.

TWENTY-SIX

The Papuan man discovered on Ina's veranda was tried under the White Women's Protection Ordinance which said that any person (the ordinance pretended that a white 'person' was as liable as a black 'person') found between the hours of 9 p.m. and daylight on the curtilage of a house in which a white woman was sleeping (here it did not pretend that a black woman was as vulnerable) had the intention to rape and would be hanged.

Looking back, it seemed unbelievable to John that such a law could have existed, and especially that it could have been written by Hubert Murray, 'the natives' friend'. It was an astonishing law because it presumed guilt. None of the black men who were arrested in its name stood any chance of a fair trial. To be charged meant hanging. Equally unbelievable perhaps, even to a cynic about Australia as John knew himself to be, it was a law ratified by the Australian parliament in 1926—a gift from Australians to their colonial black brothers.

The man on Ina's veranda was described in court as the most conscientious worker in her labour line; the one to whom she entrusted the most delicate jobs. The newspapers made much of this: his closeness to her, his familiarity. And her familiarity with him, by implication. Stephen V. (as the newspapers called him) was not allowed a lawyer to represent him. As was common practice, the judge accepted responsibility for fairness in the trial. The statement Stephen V. made to the police on the night of his arrest was his only defence. In it he said that a well-known businessman in the town (whose name the court suppressed) had given him a message ('a permit' he called it) to take to Mrs Prideaux. The written slip of paper was shown to the court. It was a piece of indecipherable scribble which Judge Hoare interpreted to have been scratched by someone who had never learnt to handle a pencil. *It was a forgery, Johnno. Done by a white hand.* The Chief Legal Officer (acting for the Crown) said the 'permit' was obviously a pathetic attempt at an alibi, probably concocted and executed by the uneducated defendant himself. *I knew my boys, Johnno, and they knew me. They would never have done such a thing. I knew the white townspeople too. I trusted them less than any Papuan.*

Witnesses were called. Andrew (whose name the judge suppressed) identified the defendant. Ina (whose name and evidence the judge suppressed although the whole town knew the story) made an impassioned speech for an acquittal on the grounds that she had not been disturbed or interfered with in the least. But her evidence carried no weight since the ordinance interpreted intention rather than achievement of rape and in any case gave hanging as the penalty for both. Other witnesses (townspeople whose names and evidence the judge also suppressed) told the court that Ina encouraged her Papuan boys to be familiar with her, teased and joked with them, and had been seen to allow them to wear shirts (which was also against the law) when working. *When handling poisonous plants, Johnno!* Furthermore, the Chief Legal Officer told the court that 'Ina Prideaux' was only an assumed name and that Ina Stocks had never been married to Andrew Prideaux.

None of the evidence helped the Papuan. The trial only lasted a morning. He was sentenced to be hanged.

Ina was outraged. Coming out onto the veranda of the rickety court house she felt as if she *had* been assaulted—not by Stephen V., but by the process of the law. She went straight down Cuthbertson Street to the Post Office and sent a telegram to the Australian Prime Minister, who had the power to suggest commutation of the sentence. The next day she received an apologetic telegram in reply. There was an election imminent and Mr Lyons did not want the Labor Party to get in. *I tore it up into the tiniest confetti and mailed it back to him, Johnno.* She wished Stanley Bruce had still been Prime Minister. He was a golfer, he might have seen sense.

On the morning of the fourth of August 1934, Ina joined the huge throbbing crowd of Papuans who lined the hills around Badili overlooking the gaol. From that height the gallows were perfectly visible although a hessian screen had been raised around them, supposedly in the name of decency. At eight o'clock the sun was already blasting, unstinting and unforgiving, on the Badili promontory. Surrounded by wailing Papuan women Ina saw the bag go over the man's head, then the rope which rucked the bag up at the side exposing half his face. Then the lever was pulled. The chanting of the crowd rose to an implacable howl. The air became thick with it. And as Stephen V. had the life wrenched out of him by simple gravity, Ina gave way too. But not audibly. Something inside her collapsed. As if there were a skin inside her skin, she wanted at that moment to step out of it, leave herself behind like an empty insect's shell. She felt unclean. She felt that the hanging of the man was an irredeemable indecency. That the stain of it would never leave the world. That his death was her crime and her death. That her soul was raped, that his was too, and that out of their shared innocence was gouged a universe of guilt.

Ina raged within herself against the entire white race on earth as she watched the body being cut down and transported away on the tray of the government truck. She turned from it and pushed her way back through the agitated crowd. She returned to the house where she packed her bags immediately, even though the boat was not due for a week. She spent that week sitting on the cane lounge on the veranda, under her monstrous staghorn, dressed and ready to go with bags and golf clubs beside her.

On the day after the hanging, the *Papuan Times* showed a photograph of Stephen Vaimuru being led to the gallows in a white lap-lap and reported him as saying, in his final words on the gallows platform: 'I am sorry for what I have done.'

Ina's hands clawed the paper, and tore that too to shreds.

TWENTY-SEVEN

In the two years leading up to Independence, work in the planning office became hectic and the tensions grew. Goffett made it known that he had no interest in remaining in the country beyond Independence, and left most of the work to John and Francis. Together they shared an ironic appreciation of the incongruities of the job. Much of their professional time they spent imagining and discussing what life would be like for post-Independence Papua New Guineans who, typically, would have been born in a primitive village, would have mediocre education, would make family homes in shanty towns on the outskirts of Moresby, would commute to work in open trucks, and would have their workplace among skyscrapers.

But the difficulties of building lifestyle quality into the plan for Waigani were as nothing, in John's mind, to the difficulties of building a relationship with Francis. John did not expect loyal devotion, and he certainly did not get it, but Francis' affections and availability were so erratic, so prone to every sort of pressure, John often wondered what it was that motivated him. Francis exercised his charm on one white woman after another, yet he kept coming back to John, apparently unable to help himself. John suspected that in the depths of Francis there lay not a great capacity for sex, but a great capacity for resentment. Francis seemed to need sex with whites as a drug, but also as a way of revenge, an act of anti-colonialism. Yet, thinking these thoughts, John knew how hypocritical it was to ascribe base motives to Francis. If Francis was using John for some deep-seated and confused psychological satisfaction, he at least was not abusing him. In bed together they showed each other a wonderful generosity. Francis never attempted the monstrosities he afflicted on his female admirers.

It was only in his lowest moments that John thought this way. He knew that no relationship in the world was found faultless in such analysis of its dark depths. He and Francis had marvellous times together—John easily recognised them as the best times of his life. Francis was his inspiration and his delight, and even in the arms of other men in Sydney or, occasionally, in Moresby, John's love for Francis grew and endured.

To escape the pressures of the planning office, John and Francis went on trips together around the country by car and plane, and on foot. 'Exploring,' they called it. *We were exploring each other, our relationship, as much as the land.* They drove out of Moresby (east, north and west) until the roads petered out. They went with male friends on drunken, twin-hulled canoe trips towards the Gulf, and in the direction of Samarai. They flew to the cool highlands where they bought English potatoes at markets nestled under pine trees and sipped hot fresh coffee in the evenings by log fires with the potatoes roasting. To Madang where the idyllic scenery of the coastal inlets eclipsed even the most romantic tropical travel brochures. And to Rabaul where volcanoes could pop out of the bay overnight and where nothing was left on open shelves because of the regular earthquakes. *In each place we fucked. It was like claiming the country together.* In his own village, out from Rabaul, Francis arranged an evening of dances especially for John's entertainment, and after the Whip Dance (where young blond-haired Tolai men leapt about and thrashed each other's ankles with long canes) a mild earthquake hit while John and Francis were making love in a thatched palm cottage *and we kept on fucking.*

But it was their walking of the Kokoda Trail that John remembered as the greatest exploration. They flew to Kokoda early one morning. There were six in the party (four Australians and two Papua New Guineans), all public servants, all male. John had been in training for weeks, climbing up and down Burns Peak each evening, lugging a haversack which contained an increasing number of heavy stones. He had also studied the maps of the trail. On the plan maps the track appeared as a twisting dotted line linking village to village half way across Papua—a long way to walk but not too forbidding. On the elevation maps however the trail was shown as the progress of an ant up and down the teeth of a comb. In total the trail from Kokoda back to the outskirts of Moresby rose and fell 29 000 feet (equivalent to climbing up and down Mount Everest from sea level) and it wriggled for 93 kilometres. They intended to do it in five days. That was the most time available to one member of the party, who had to return to work for a conference. Their Islander plane took off eastwards from Moresby airport and climbed into the grey dawn. Above Kokoda the plane dipped down into the valley through a wispy hole in the early morning cloud lying thickly over the airstrip.

The dotted lines on the maps gave little clue to the actual terrain they would enter. John found that the Kokoda Trail was even worse than he had imagined or seen in Parer's horror photographs and Johnston's *New Guinea Diary*. Even without the Japanese the Kokoda Trail was a nightmare: the constant draining battles against the tyranny of gravity up the sheer ridges where the knees faltered and the breath died in the chest; then the slippery, hellish descents where the ankles gave and the toes were crushed maddeningly in the boots. *Dante's descent through Hell was a stroll by comparison.* On the first night they slept in a village above the Kokoda Gap, at 5 000 feet, and in the morning looked out on a level with light planes flying above the clouds. Later that day John stood on a ridge beyond Templeton's Crossing and turned full circle. What a scene! Myriad mountain tops, a countless crowd of craning green heads, serried and jostling to a serrated horizon. Giants dwarfing other giants. Topography gone troppo. (Troppography?) Mad nodules eruptive on the earth's skin, a rash of mountains, seven, ten, fourteen thousand feet high. *But beside my hand, on a leaf shaped like a green trumpet blast, the most exquisite blue butterfly, giant, and frail as gauze.*

In a rushing stream at the foot of the ridge they lay together out of sight of the others with the spangled water whirring around them.

On the third day one of the Australians tossed his boots over a cliff and sat down in the middle of the track. He wept. 'I can't do it,' he repeated. He lay back on his unremoved pack and covered his eyes with the palms of his hands. They had to tie a rope around his waist and drag him along. 'We can't just leave you here, Geoff.' He shuffled, bare-footed. That evening in the thatched guest house in Nauro village, Francis took off his own boots and emptied his toenails out of his socks. His toes were a pulp of blisters. 'You should have trained, you mad bastard,' John told him. They filled his socks with antibiotic powder the next day, and lightened his pack. He hobbled on in agony. *Dear God. And it wasn't even war time.*

Along the Kokoda Trail, John consciously recognised history. In the jungle on either side of the track, in the *chiaroscuro* of light dripping through myriad leaves, he could make out the camouflaged faces of soldiers. In the torrid silences of moss forests he could hear the stealthy foot-falls, and the club-club of fearful hearts. Coming up to a rise in the track, a false crest, he noticed the depression in the mulch where a foxhole would have been and where a gun would have clattered at him. There were bullet cases and the occasional helmet or bayonet still able to be discovered in the tangle of undergrowth beside the track. John wondered how far he needed to stray from the dotted line of the trail before he came across dead bodies, skeletons by now. They were there; they had to be. He could feel that they were. A *live* Japanese soldier had been discovered that year in the jungle on the north coast. He had been bloody glad to hear that the war had ended, even though it happened thirty years before.

They slogged on to the finish. At Ower's Corner in the mountains at the Moresby end of the trail, the party was met by a friend with a car-load of beer and champagne. *Dear Christ, the stuff never tasted so good.* John and Francis toasted each other, poured it over each other. The whole group joined in, bathed in froth and alcohol. The man with the rope around his waist was liberated. (The rope had been unnecessary on the fourth day—his spirits had risen once the end of the ordeal was in sight, but he had worn it just the same, as a self-imposed badge of shame, it seemed.) They took photographs of each other smiling with their arms about each other's shoulders. *We were magnificent creatures. We had survived.*

To John the survival of the Kokoda Trail seemed tantamount to passing through a torrid initiation rite; he and Francis were clan mates. Later that night, down on the coast in hot Moresby, under the *chopper-chopper* of the bedroom fan, he and Francis celebrated again, feeling the incredible tautness of their track-tuned bodies, the hardness of their calf muscles, the leanness of their buttocks. 'Just don't touch my bloody toes,' Francis wailed.

It wasn't long before they were laughing about the entire Kokoda Trail experience.

'You didn't walk the Kokoda Trail, mate. You hobbled it.'

'The Cock-odour Trail?'

'The Cock-ardour Trail.'

'Cock harder?'

'What about when the cigarette papers ran out and we rolled them in toilet paper?'

'And bandaids.'

'Or that bloody bottle of pink-and-white humbugs.'

'With one black-and-white one at the bottom.'

They rewarded themselves with a boiled sweet at each ridge. Everyone was thinking about who would get the prize of the black one.

'Then bloody Alan disappeared for a while, just before Ua-Ulle Creek.'

'We thought he was having a shit.'

'And at the next ridge—Imita Ridge, it was—the black-and-white one had gone.'

'We nearly killed the bastard.'

'I really did want to kill him. I premeditated his murder.'

John had been lowered by the physical agony and mental torture of the trail to a baser, simpler plane of logic; he didn't care about the morals or the consequences of killing. He had come down the Golden Staircase choking with rage. Then he had waded neck-deep in a creek holding his haversack above his head and had plotted the murder of an Australian colleague because he had eaten a humbug.

'We were going mad, *poro*.'

'You might have been, with your toes falling off. I was perfectly sane. *War-sane*.'

When they reached Ower's Corner and the road which stretched down to Moresby, all the madness had dissipated.

'We did it, mate. We survived.'

In spite of the traumas, or perhaps because of them, John internalised the map of the Kokoda Trail. He carried it inside his head—a determined dotted line across the jagged centre of an unforgiving land. Unforgiving, yes. But not unpredictable. Papua New Guinea was a constant, a wilderness which re-produced itself over and over, celebrated itself in immutable growth, self-regeneration. It was a powerhouse with no interest in progress or change. It did not wish to be or produce other than it was. It was satisfied with its own perfection. Men, like occasional ants, walked on dotted lines over it, and it shrugged them off. Especially town planners. In John's mind the map of the trail became the blueprint and contract of his relationship with Francis. They had shared an incredible experience. An ascent into Hell. A topological reversal. It bound him to Francis and to the country. He felt he knew something of the heart of them both, and something of his own heart.

'You know what the soldiers called the stairs they dug into the side of Imita Ridge in the war? The Golden Staircase. Golden because it ran golden with the diarrhoea of thousands of sick Australian soldiers.' He couldn't get that out of his head. *Shitting their hearts out.*

But for Francis the conquest of the trail was only partly a binding. He resented the loss of his toenails. 'The trail turned me into a woman,' he complained. 'To match my arse.' He was very touchy about the blackness of his buttocks. 'Sitting on a bloody seat does it to you. Studying does it. Every student at the University has an arse blacker than the rest of his body.

131

Every public servant has too. From rubbing on seats all day. That's what we get from Western culture. Black, black arses. Like village women who sit all the time.'

When he was drunk with John he would go floppy as a cloth doll, the sinews seeming to collapse in him. He would lie around on furniture or on the floor, happily defeated by drink, by the world, smilingly careless about his own submission. But in the company of women he was different. He had a reputation for getting drunk then beating them.

'I can't help it. I *have* to beat them.'

Always white women. Women who could not resist him.

'Your cock is a Moresby legend, mate,' John would say, hurt.

And Francis would smile with such charm. 'I'm a tragic victim of culture clash, *poro*. That's my excuse.'

John indulged Francis, and in doing so indulged himself. Some of his white friends were of the opinion that he was heading for trouble. He ignored their quiet warnings.

The riot which had been backdrop to their first night together became known by all as the Waigani Riot. The route the rioters took went out of the Boroko shopping centre, along Sir Hubert Murray Drive, and turned left into Waigani Road. The rioters smashed the windows of cars all along Waigani Road until they were finally stopped by police just past the Wards Road intersection, at exactly the point where Independence Drive was surveyed to start. Perhaps it was only the Town Planning Department who saw the irony. They laughed and shook their heads. The name changes came thick and fast over coffee: 'Why-Can't-We? Drive'; 'Where-Are-We? Drive'; 'Into Penance Drive'. There was even a set of traffic lights intended for that intersection, although what the rioters saw was a patch of spindly eucalypt scrub bristling with armed police behind a barricade of flood-lit lock-up vans. 'It has started,' Francis had said, pointing out to John—unnecessarily as it happened—that ironically the rioters (mainly New Guinea highlanders) had been protesting *against* Independence. They were conservatives, he explained bitterly. They did not want to join with their Papuan brothers. They did not want the country to have to stand on its own two feet. They wanted Australia to stay *mama* to its *pikinini*.

On Independence Day a long procession of dancers bobbed and shimmied down Independence Drive in a belated continuation of the route of the riot. Highlanders, Sepiks, Mekeos, Motuans, Tolais, Trobrianders, Gulf men dressed in everything from bird of paradise plumes to dogs' teeth, from Chinese-store tinsel to mud. They vibrated barefooted on the 1.1 kilometres of scorching bitumen followed by Prince Charles in an open Land-Rover and the Chief Minister with the cabinet and other dignitaries in new white limousines. The crowds on either side pressed forward like the waves of a colourful sea. The lights at the intersection were working magnificently, although the official procession took no notice of them. The police cycle outriders went through on green, the Prince on orange, and the Chief Minister and cabinet on red. The cameras of the world's media whirred as the newly-designed red, black and gold flag was raised. The Prince ('*pikinin bilong Kwin*,' as he was called in Pidgin English, the new *lingua franca*) read his speech and declared the Waigani Government Centre open. *We thought he looked simply stunning in his short-sleeved safari suit.*

Even John and Francis were part of the procession. There was a limousine assigned to Architecture and Planning. None of the architects wanted to be in it, and Goffett had taken his golden handshake one week before Independence Day, so it was John and Francis together, stalled to an ant's pace on six-lane Independence Drive with the flag-waving crowds hard by outside the windows. The Enga chauffeur turned the air-conditioning to what seemed like the deep-freeze-polar setting, but he also couldn't keep his fingers off the electric window buttons. '*Pressim i go up. Pressim i go down.*' The two men were in stitches on the back seat. John pressed the switch of his red bow tie and it whirred as the limousine windows danced crazily up and down. The chauffeur turned his head around, grinning at the madness of it all. 'It's Taxi Number 33,' Francis spluttered delightedly. He was red-eyed and sweating, high on betelnut and intoxicated by the occasion.

Later that afternoon, way out past the carpark, and past the reach of the new Australian Embassy's long shadow, the Architect's Division hosted a *mu-mu* (a barbecue, some of the rigid expatriates called it). A great quantity of luxuriously cold keg beer was consumed. By sundown, when the topping earth was dug away and the sugar bags and banana leaves removed from the *mu-mu* pit to expose the steaming earth oven crammed with chicken and pig meat and vegetables, John was pissed. He stood in the pink sunset on rough ground beside a tortured-looking eucalypt with a pale chicken-leg in his hand, and surveyed the five incongruous skyscrapers sticking up in front of him, pink-washed in the last light. It was madness. *My madness. Australian madness.* A new plastic heart for a tropical country. He gave the bow tie an idiotic whir.

He knew exactly where he stood. He could have placed an exact cross on any of the plans in his office.

X—YOU ARE HERE.

He stood where a future development, perhaps in ten years time, would erect a garage for the extended motor pool. In the glare of the porta-floods as the darkness rolled in, he watched Francis Tapukai turn the charm of his laughing, blood-shot eyes onto one of the Embassy secretaries. Then, while he was at the keg re-filling his glass, Francis and the woman disappeared. *So what. It was Independence Day, wasn't it?*

John staggered into the dark and tried to find his way back to the carpark. There should have been nothing difficult about that, but in his inebriated state he kept coming up against twisted tree trunks and mounds of bulldozed earth. He tried to remember the plan of the government office site (he knew it like the back of his hand when sober) but in the dark his course zig-zagged woefully, and he fell, or at least he thought he fell (he was sure the next morning that he remembered falling) into an open stormwater drain about the safety of which he had given personal assurance to the Government Architect in a memo two years before.

TWENTY-EIGHT

In the Hydro albums John saw a photograph of the cures pool in its heyday. A group of women in swimsuits and caps sat on a strip of sand with the mountain scrub and several large sandstone boulders behind them. Off to the side was the surface of the spring-fed pool.

'It's still there,' the girl behind the desk informed him. 'Down towards the bluff. About a half-hour's walk.'

What the hell. Kill or cure.

He asked the girl for a map of the hotel's walking tracks. She gave him an inky, blurred sheet. He studied the dotted lines indicating the trails around the cliff tops. He vaguely remembered walking them as a child but he could not remember the cures pool.

He climbed to his room to put on his heavy coat, then came back down. Outside he went around by the tennis courts and found the windy stairs leading below the hotel. The track starting there took him over the drop on which the Hydro teetered. Looking back up after only a few minutes of rough downhill walking, he could see the building at its most spectacular, a zig-zag of joined buildings really, strung out along the cliff top. It looked like something from a European post card, provided he closed his eyes to the scaffolding for the new work and the rubbish thrown down by the workmen: old paint tins, boxes, pieces of guttering which littered the escarpment. The track too was in need of repair. The photographs had shown a horse and buggy gaily driving but the track was now just wide enough for one person, and even so it was a painful descent.

John's ankles were wrenched by exposed roots and deep runnels gouged out by rainwaters.

It's a distraction from my guts' pain.

He knew as he went that he would have trouble getting back up. The track was steep. His strength would run out. But he kept going. He pushed aside scrubby bushes overgrowing the track. He sent loose shaly rocks tumbling. One consolation was that here in the sheltering scrub the wind was absent.

At a turn in the track he stopped and looked behind. He thought he had heard someone following. He listened for several moments. Silence. He kept on, then halted again. Was that a grey shadow in the trees behind? He pressed on, feeling the sweat in his groin.

At last he heard water trickling where a dell opened out and he stood on a flat expanse of sand with low bushes growing over it. He recognised the sandstone boulders and realised that he was in the middle of the cures pool, in the middle of where it had been in its heyday. It was now entirely choked with sand across which lay, in a fan of trickling channels, the spring water once advertised as so efficacious. He bent down, sweating inside his coat, and scooped up a palmful of the water. It was cold. He looked at its discoloration and wondered about pollution, drains, septic tanks, new housing estates back up the mountain beyond the bush. He put the water to his lips. It tasted all right. Bushy, Australian, nothing exotic. *Australian water: hard and tea-coloured.* It had a brown scrubby smell which reminded him of his childhood.

He could hear a waterfall nearby, a dripping rather than a torrent, and he pushed the spindly bushes aside to see the curved brick wall, two metres high, four metres long, joining two rocky ledges. This wall, which had originally created the pool, had also ultimately destroyed it as the sand was dammed up too. Now there was no cures pool, just a large load of sand.

John pushed on through the line of scrub and received a shock when he saw that immediately beyond the bushes there was a rock ledge, then the precipice plunging away. He was on the brink of a cliff. Within six or seven metres of the cures pool as he had seen it in the photograph, and screened from view by the backdrop of scrub, was the abyss. *Perhaps it was designed that way. If the pool didn't cure you, you could toss yourself off the edge.* But he received a bigger start when one of the rocky outcrops along the ledge moved and turned into a man in a grey overcoat.

'Christ. You gave me a shock!'

The man had a reddish face. His hands were in the pockets of the overcoat. He did not remove them. He seemed nervous— not about the fact that he was standing on the brink of a three hundred metre drop, but because someone had surprised him there.

'Amazing spot,' the man said, after a moment's hesitation. 'Perfect view.' As if he were a customer browsing in a postcard shop. He gazed back out across the plunging gulf.

John looked out into the great amphitheatre of cliff faces, but immediately felt himself beginning to sway. The drop was horrifying. The ledge on which he stood seemed to tilt under his feet. The cliff face further up, with the hotel beetling above it, began to lurch. John stepped backwards.

The man turned his chubby form towards him. 'People have suicided here,' he said, too cheerfully. 'Can't see it myself. A gun'd be much quicker.' The man stepped forward suddenly. One leather street shoe was right at the lip of the ledge. He craned over, looking down. 'They'd have splattered right there somewhere. Bayoneted on a tree trunk, probably.'

Seeing the toe of the man's shoe kissing the brink, John had the terrible thought that this odd-ball might have it in mind to slip over, in a jovial, accidental way. He wondered whether he shouldn't be talking the man out of his fascination with peering over the edge.

'You're not thinking of jumping, are you?'

The man walked unperturbed along the ledge, laughing loudly. 'Been there, done that, mate. I was in Vietnam.' He stepped past John. He had a craggy head which he held high. He pulled a cap out of his pocket and put it on. 'I reminisce though. See you later,' he said, pushing his way into the bushes.

TWENTY-NINE

Ina left Port Moresby on the first boat out after Stephen Vaimuru's hanging. She put it all behind her—the gardens, the golf course, the lieutenant-governor. On the veranda, with the ship waiting at the wharf, Andrew begged her to stay, but she couldn't. She felt betrayed by Papua and by Andrew.

'I need a long holiday,' she told him. 'A very long holiday.' Knowing what his response would be, she suggested he come with her.

He looked across the mangrove-strewn beach towards the ship. 'There's a Depression back there, The world is smoking more cigarettes than ever during the hard times.' He had four tobacco plantations. He could not leave them.

She put the strap of her golf bag over her shoulder. 'I don't think I mean to "go finish", I only want a long furlough. Time enough to forget.'

He bent and lifted her suitcase.

From the wharf he waved up to her on the deck of the ship. He wore a new helmet and a spotless fawn suit. *He looked wonderful, Johnno. The tropics suited him.* She turned her back on him and on Papua, and went down to her cabin before the ship departed.

She was thirty-nine (though she said thirty-four) when she came to the Hydro in 1934. She stayed there for a total of twenty-two years. Prideaux paid for it all. And the nightmares persisted all that time. *They began on the night following poor Vaimuru's hanging, Johnno. They stayed with her on the ship. They followed her to the Hydro. They were with her in* whatever bed she slept. Their theme varied only slightly. She would wake, or think she woke, to find a vague, horrifying scaffold at the end of her bed (a vision moulded out of the darkness) and on it a black man would be hanging, a black naked body with a bag over its head. The rope would part. He would be falling forwards, dead arms flailing towards her. Sometimes the rope would not part and the whole gallows would be falling forward. Sometimes the corpse would howl through the bag, and she would wake to her own voice howling. *I mentioned nothing of it to doctors, or to your parents.* And on every occurrence it seemed to get a fraction closer to her in its falling.

I was the receptacle for a whole colony's guilt. I carried its waste away. I expect they felt cleaner in Moresby once Vaimuru and I had gone. When she thought of Andrew, she thought of a man in a fawn suit married to Papua, while she was married to Death.

I stayed in my cabin all the way to Sydney, Johnno. I didn't even go up on deck when the steamer passed under the new Harbour Bridge.

Ina made her first contact with her children two months after arriving at the Hydro. She hired a car to take her through Lithgow and Oberon to Mount Werong. She had heard that Little Tom had bought a property there and had moved from Sydney to live on it. She expected something grand: a homestead, sheep and cattle perhaps. The hired car drove higher into the mountains. The grey weather became chillier. She looked out the window at the smooth silvery trunks of *Eucalyptus pauciflora* and *E. dalrympleana*. Alpine, close-growing, blue-grey leaves limp as dead men's fingers. The car bumped up the last winding miles of the rough road and entered a fall of snow. *It was October! I was glad I'd brought my fur coat.* She wondered why Little Tom had chosen such a commerce-forsaken place.

She soon found out. Mount Werong was not a town, just a heavily-timbered collection of allotments. The road wound between trees and passed a variety of tin shacks and timber humpies, all nestled back in the forest. There were white men standing outside each of them, watching the car go by. They seemed to have nothing to do but watch. Her driver stopped and asked for directions.

'Tom's place? Just keep going. You can't miss it. It's on the left. You'll see the car parked there. Only car in the settlement.'

They grinned and waved Ina away. But when the driver pulled up at Tom's place Ina could not believe her eyes. Twenty metres from the road a car was parked beneath tall trees. From the back of the car a chimney-pipe stood up. From the side of the car was built a lean-to shed.

It was not a comfortable meeting. *I was nervous, Johnno. I kept wanting to cry.* Ina sat on a bench made from the back seat of the car, and watched her children who watched her in return with great suspicion. The nineteen-year-old girl in baggy pants studied her in an uncomprehending way, while the seventeen-year-old boy, seemingly more certain and more hostile, was expressionless. Little Tom talked, enough to be polite, in a resentful way, challenging her with his upraised chin to comment on his reduced state.

'So I shouldn't have left the tobacco industry when I did, should I?' The memory rankled. The anger and hurt were barely concealed in his voice. 'We've done all right here though. I don't give a damn how long this Depression goes on. I can pan enough gold out of the creek to get us by.'

She would not have called it 'getting by'. The shack had a stamped earth floor. The children's clothes (well, they were hardly children any more) were eccentric and grubby. Men's clothes. Cast-offs. They did not fit properly.

'. . . So how was I to know that car sales would be so heavily hit? I had a dealership in Cremorne—very good class of area. If I'd just had a bit longer to establish . . .' He had been over it a thousand times before.

'Perhaps Andrew could set you up again,' she ventured. 'Like you did for him.'

Little Tom shook his head and stuck his chin out. 'I like it here,' he said.

They gave her tea and biscuits. When the girl offered her a

biscuit from the tin-lid tray in one hand, she reached out the other towards Ina's throat. Ina thought she was going to caress her, but the girl just wanted to feel the fur of the woman's coat collar.

'Why don't you come and stay with me a while, Louise? For a holiday. And you too, Cliffie. Would you like that?'

The girl said she might, and looked at her father. He shrugged. But the youth got up and walked out the low door. He didn't come back. He wasn't around when Ina got into the hired car to leave.

'I've told them all about you,' Little Tom said, with a foot on the running board and a hand on the window sill.

Inside the car she said nothing.

'Cliffie hasn't coped with it,' he added, as the driver moved the ignition switch. 'It's poisoned him.'

Little Tom slapped the body of the car twice with the palm of his hand as it moved away. Ina understood it as a salute to his own undying pride and selfishness. He turned his back and headed for the shack.

Ina found the Hydro rather a comfort to get back to after that. *I needed loneliness, Johnno. I could lose myself among the crowds of guests.* She saw Louise twice a year from then on, sometimes more. Cliffie, she never saw. He went with his father to Queensland. They ran a service station on the coast. She imagined them in overalls with their hands blackened by grease, putting petrol in people's cars outside an oily garage with the sun beating down somewhere near Southport. *They didn't need me, Johnno. They were too fierce and resentful. And I knew I didn't need them. But Andrew: that was different.* She often wished she could write to someone and say: Take care of him. Probably a black someone was doing that anyway. He never mentioned any such thing in his letters, but she supposed he was playing out the Errol Flynn-style dreams she had always sensed in him. And because he did not refer to such matters, she in her letters did not mention the nights when she wrestled on her bed with Stephen Vaimuru in dark secrecy, fending him off and fending him off.

Sixteen years in Papua! My body wouldn't re-acclimatise. My eyes wouldn't. Sometimes she craved the heat, the colours, the mad spurts of growth. She bought two more fur coats for the winters and pretended to herself that perspiring had been a wonderful experience. In summer she swam in the cures pool and stretched out on the sand beside it, imagining that having a good dark tan was healthy and would make her feel better. But she did not feel better, she remained nightmare-driven. Only when she took up golf again did she find a modicum of release. Quite soon she was playing daily, obsessively, as if swinging a club with the regularity of a metronome would erase the fear of Vaimuru's body descending over her.

She made the Blackheath course her home. She was champion there five years running. She travelled a great deal, played in tournaments around the state. She began writing a column which proved popular and was syndicated in the country newspapers. It was called 'Rub of the Green, with Ina Stocks'. She filled it with golfing hints, lore, whimsy and philosophy, all directed towards Australian women. She always headed with an item calculated to deter male readers. Something like: 'How To Clean Your Two-Toned Shoes, Ladies', or 'How To Bend Gracefully At the Hole, Keeping Your Hem Straight'. After that she would launch into the subversive stuff: 'Why The Male Anatomy Is Unsuited To Golf', or 'Simple Dishes To Cook At Home To Give You More Time On The Fairways'.

The mail she received at the Hydro each week was enormous. 'Dear Ina, Last Wednesday I played a scratch-round three strokes better than my husband's best. How can I possibly break the news to him? Signed, Handicapped.' She liked to answer with a witticism: 'Dear Handicapped, Find a good lie. Ina.'

Her life became golf. She wrote for it, travelled for it, made it into a paying business. In 1938 she became nationally famous (at least among golfers) for two sayings: 'Please don't bomb the greens of England, Mr Hitler,' and 'Let's hope the bombs don't land in the bunkers.' The latter led to a column in the major city newspapers. 'Shots from the Bunker, Ina Stocks' Column.' It ran for the length of the war.

THIRTY

John observed the changes in Port Moresby in the years following Independence. The town turned itself inside out. The Papua New Guineans moved into the jobs and houses that the whites abandoned. The roads deteriorated. The suburban lawns turned to bare compounds. The executive residences had thatched lean-tos thrown up against their side walls. Immaculate shop fronts were gradually discoloured with the grubby fingerprints, handprints and shoulderprints of the people who reclaimed their town by touching it where previously they would have been *raused* away. Moresby regressed to being a big grubby village, shiny with the patina of barefooted, barehanded usage; and John liked it that way. The squatter settlements swelled on all sides of the town. From them the rascal gangs raided the wealthier suburbs. John had to fight off an attempt by the government to build a six-foot-high cyclone wire fence around the new executive house he moved into in Lawes Road.

But it was the cars he liked best. To him they really showed the local signature on progress. On Sir Hubert Murray Highway the ratio of white drivers to black had been reversed. Before Independence only one in ten drivers was Papua New Guinean. After Independence it was rare to see a white person behind the wheel. And in taking over ownership of the cars, the locals applied what Francis called 'their own identity' to them. Cars were painted over with house paint in village motifs. Broken car windows were replaced with sheets of corrugated iron cut to fit. Or cars were driven without windscreens, without boot-lids, without fenders, full of happy co-owners wearing dark sunglasses, who made a point of taking right-of-way over white drivers. John gave way gladly. He celebrated their version of civilisation. He applauded their refashioning of modernity in their own image. He supported their exorcism of the colonial past. In his identification with their breaking of the old colonial rules he felt at home, non-alien.

Like a minority of other Australians who chose to stay behind, John considered taking out Papua New Guinean citizenship. It would have been a way of showing his loyalty to the country, but he decided against it. The benefits he had as an expatriate—his big salary and his annual repatriated leave breaks—he could not give up. Francis was the indirect beneficiary of the big salary. John paid for the wonderful times they had together, and he delighted in keeping Francis' flat extravagantly stocked with food, alcohol and erotic curios. It was for Francis that John decided to stay Australian.

John thought long and hard about changing his name to something like 'John Warbat' to emphasise his commitment to the country. But each year, on his four week leave break in Sydney, he experienced an uncontrollable madness to escape all loyalties—an almost self-destructive urge for abandonment. Powered by coke or amyls or whatever drug his friends had at the time, he surrendered to the glittering, brittle world of the Sydney scene, wearing at his neck the trademark of his increasing turmoil and confusion—the whirring red bow tie.

'I went crazy in Sydney again, Francis,' he would apologise on his return.

'That's all right, *poro*. We all need to go crazy.'

'But I really went crazy this time.'

'What did you do?'

'I paid for someone.'

'A *pamuk*?'

'An Aborigine. I felt sorry for him. He reminded me of you. He needed the money.'

Over the years Francis lived with several white women in his government house at Hohola. Most of them moved out when he started beating them.

'I don't really beat the women,' he explained to John on one occasion. 'I just beat the whiteness in them.'

'Why don't you beat me, then?'

'Oh, *poro*. There's too much bloody black in you, isn't there.'

Ah, those long Papuan days. Driving in the early morning cool. That wild celery smell in large-leafed, long-leafed groves beside the roadway. Remember the smell? Fecund. That was the word I always thought of. Then bouncing rides along swampy tracks, through tangles of mangroves to out-of-the-way beaches. Remember Bootless Inlet? Taurama? The photographs? You floating naked. You bending over the camp-fire naked. You showing off, Tolai spear at the ready. God, I loved you. Was lost and found in you. Gaped and burnt for you, ached to disappear in you, to be buried and born in you, to take you and burn with you, wearing perspiration and clinging sand, the sun in my eyes and throat, the searing caress, lifting my head and howling at the blue. Liu liu liu.

In the dry season of 1984 Francis' mother died. John paid for the air fares and they flew together to Rabaul. They reached the village on the back of a truck late at night, and walked up a dark sandy street full of wailing and shrieking. A warm, salt wind blew from the beach through the coconut palms. To John the clashing of the fronds resembled applause from skeletal hands.

Much of Francis' time would be taken up by the ceremonies which continued day and night all weekend, but he took John to see his father as soon as they arrived and the three sat on the bamboo veranda of the house for a long time in the midst of the wailing.

The old man politely interrupted his grief to welcome John, but was uninterested in conversation. He held his son's hand and stared into the night. Above his reddened eyes slanted a military-style slouched hat.

'An Australian soldier gave it to him after the war,' Francis explained. 'I always wanted to wear it when I was a boy. But he never let me.'

The old man began to sing in a shaky guttural voice.

'He wore it on the day he took me to the mission school at Kokopo. I didn't want to go to school. I kept trying to run back home. He grabbed me and beat me. I never forgave the hat.'

'Why did the Australian give it to him?'

'He saved his life. He found him in our garden lands with his leg off. The Japanese bombs had hit the garden and the soldier was lying there. Father bandaged his leg with banana leaves and a coconut husk. The soldier kept sending presents from Australia for years after the war. Cigars in boxes, long pants, shirts, blankets, and then the hat. Father loved the presents more than anything. "If you go to school you will have cigars in boxes," he always said to me. My friends in the village who didn't have to go to school called my father "The Australian". Their fathers thought up the name. All the men wanted the cigars but he never shared them. "Find your own broken soldier," he told them. He hurt my mother saying things like that.'

'And was the soldier's name "Francis"?' John asked.

'Ha. How did you know, *poro?*'

Later that night, stretched out on the floor in a partitioned room of the stuffy bamboo house, John listened to the clashing applause of the palm fronds above the roof and knew that no new citizenship, no new name, no cosmetic change could demonstrate his loyalty. He couldn't marry Francis to show his love or his need. He couldn't be reborn in a new skin. He had no rights, and guilt was no justification for staying. Yet the massive burden of identity which he felt within urged him to stay. He felt he belonged and he could not understand why.

Back in Moresby he arrived home to find a large hole in his study wall. A rascal gang had removed the air-conditioner and come through the hole to burgle the house. His expensive hi-fi equipment was taken. So too were his golf clubs, his camera and all his clothes (including a garbage bag full of dirty underwear). To carry most of the loot out the gang had taken his set of designer suitcases and the backpack which he had used on the Kokoda Trail and kept for sentimental reasons. Even his leather jacket (only worn on trips to Sydney) had gone, along with several unique New Guinea-print shirts. He imagined a thirteen-year-old rascal sweating in leather in one of the squatter settlements, and the rest of the gang parading the Moresby streets in his Hara-hara shirts. But he did nothing about it. *That was fair enough. Things I needed I took from their country. I did not resent them taking some small part back.* The gang had taken all the rock music cassettes, but had left him his precious Tolai love songs. The rascals were not interested in tradition, it seemed.

John had no sleep that night. He lay in his double bed and thought about his future. He knew he should come to the conclusion that this was the time to go. He tried to tell himself it was wrong for him to stay longer. It was not his country. He was Chief Town Planner now and he knew there was a Papua New Guinean who could do the job equally well, if not better. But to resign for Francis Tapukai's sake, for the country's sake, meant leaving the country and Francis. At work the next morning he wrote out his letter of resignation, knowing he was being dishonest, quite certain that it would be rejected. It would go to the Director of Public Works and then to the Minister, Ted Bunani, who was no fool. John heard nothing for a week. Then came a phone call from the Minister's secretary inviting him to have a round of golf with the Minister.

They played one weekday morning at the new course, out past the new Government House at Waigani. John played badly with a hired set of sticks. The old joke about making sure you did not play better than the boss never became relevant. Mr Bunani, a short, fat man in a massive pair of grey shorts which came down over his knees, treated the rules of golf as he treated advice from his departmental heads. He ignored them. Chuckling and kicking his ball back onto the fairway of the first hole, he said to John, 'I got your letter. Very nicely written.' Giggling, and uprooting a small tree which was in his way in the rough on the third, he added, 'I am not accepting your resignation, John.' In the rough on the seventh, and swinging an iron like a *sarif* knife in order to cut a swathe in the grass in front of him, he roared with laughter, 'I am allowed to do this. I'm the Minister for Works.' Replacing his ball a metre closer the hole than his mark on the ninth green, he confided, 'You're the only man for the job, John. You can't go. I won't let you. Who else can hold Planning together, eh?'

They had lunch in the clubhouse at departmental expense. The Minister drank six beers to John's two. 'I carried Australian soldiers on the Kokoda Trail, you know,' Bunani said. 'I was only fourteen. I probably carried your father.'

My father was in the Navy, but never mind.

Bunani looked at his gold watch. 'You better be getting back to work, John.' He waved John up from his seat with a flapping hand. 'I have every faith in you. And stop worrying about Francis. He can't do your job. He is unreliable. There is localisation, and there is localisation. Eh?' The Minister squirted with laughter again and wiped his face with a serviette. 'We are westernising. We need westerners.' He flapped some more, waving John away. The meeting was over.

Getting into his car out in the burning carpark, John saw six cartons of beer piled on the back seat. A present, he supposed, from Mr Bunani, at departmental expense.

Soon after the golfing match with Bunani, John's relationship with Francis took a turn for the worse. It was the 22nd of December, 1984. John remembered the date because it was impossible to forget what he went and did on the Christmas Day after it. The 22nd was the eve of his departure for leave in Sydney. He had a bottle of Glenfiddich and an exquisite carving of coupling snakes for Francis' Christmas present. He also had a shell money necklace for Jill.

Jill was yet another Australian woman Francis had attracted by *warbat* or whatever means to live with Francis in his Hohola house. She too, or so it seemed to John, was a fervent inverted racist like himself. She had changed her name to Jill Warwarup (from Jill Hall) after Independence. She had an official white husband who was an anthropologist at the University, but maritally-speaking, Jill had opted for some original research of her own.

She hurt me, as they all did, but I was determined not to be a bitch about it. What right had I?

148

John turned off Hohola Road into the dirt road which led to Francis' place. He knew something was wrong the minute he turned into the drive. There was a crowd of people in the front yard, standing among the hibiscus bushes and traveller's palms looking up at the lighted windows. It wasn't until John stopped the car motor that he heard the crashing and screaming.

John had long known that any sort of domestic argument attracted a crowd of neighbours in Moresby. And it was usually a vocal, amused crowd. But this one wasn't. They were not used to a mixed-race melee where a black man was beating up a white woman. White man on black woman, yes. But not the reverse.

John rushed up the stairs to the balcony. If the argument had been black on black the door would have been open, the woman would have arranged it that way to ensure maximum publicity for the injustice she suffered. But the door was shut. He banged on it several times. There was no let up in the fracas inside. He had to break the fly screen wire beside the door to get his hand through the louvres and around to the inside door knob.

When John finally broke in he found Jill Warwarup in the bedroom, tied to the bed while Francis thrashed her with a belt.

On the floor in all rooms, like detritus left after a tidal wave, was a carpet of empty bottles, empty wine casks, empty cigarette packets, empty betelnut husks. Francis was paralytically drunk; clinically, John imagined, he should not have been able to stand. Jill too was practically unconscious. She did not have the awareness to rearrange her sarong as he pushed Francis away and untied the twine on her wrists and ankles. She grunted as he wiped at the vomit on the bed around her head, and at the mat of vomit in her hair. He asked her if she was all right, and seeing the terrible welts on her stomach and face, he turned on Francis.

Francis was leaning against the door post, not watching him, just looking unsteadily at the ceiling with his chin wavering up and down and his head against the jamb. He had a drunken, self-satisfied smile on his face, and John had the idea that there was a piece of music going through his mind, and that he was loving listening to it. His head nodded, swivelling on the fulcrum of his long neck, and John saw the Adam's apple beautifully defined in profile and hit it with his fist as hard as he could. He had never hit anyone like that before. He was impressed with how much it hurt his hand.

Francis fell down. In amazement he looked back at John from the floor. On his back, raised on his elbows, he slithered backwards, pushing through the party flotsam. When he was far enough off to feel safe he struggled to his feet. 'You colonialist bastard,' he slurred thickly, and crashed his way through the wire screen door.

John later decided that his biggest mistake that night was made when, at that point, he turned back to Jill. Not out of concern for her condition (he would regretfully admit to himself) but because he was fascinated—obscenely excited was closer to the truth—by the sight of her body: forked, dishevelled, entirely gaping with a worn, wet look about it. Francis had used her, had turned loose his private riot onto her. It made John feel sick, and terribly jealous.

The sound of the car motor did not register in his consciousness until it was well started and on its way. He ran out to the balcony and saw the neighbours peering down the road. Some of them looked back up at him with amused pity on their faces. The Papua New Guinean had escaped in the Australian husband's car! That lifted the domestic row to a more comical level for them.

But Francis did not get far. At a corner just before the Hohola shops he ran into a child crossing the road under a street light. She bounced off the car and into the gutter. Somehow Francis had the presence of mind to continue driving to the Hohola police station. Three policemen bundled him into a van and brought him back to the scene of the accident. The girl was lying in the gutter with one leg bent at an obscene angle. The crowd which had gathered around her was so threatening, the three constables got back into the van and returned to the station. Eventually the ambulance and a large number of police vehicles arrived at the scene from Boroko. By that time the man whose blood (or money) the crowd were calling for was already charged with driving under the influence of liquor, driving under the influence of betelnut, driving in a dangerous manner, and (something John hadn't known about) driving without a licence.

John put off his flight to Sydney. The police wanted him for questioning. He had to say the car was stolen, or else they were going to charge him too, as an accomplice. It added another charge to Francis' sheet: theft of a motor vehicle. John hardly dared go to see him in the lock up the next day, but when he did Francis greeted him with the usual coyness and charm, as if he had been merely naughty.

'I'm sorry, *poro*,' Francis said. 'They told me they locked your car up in the yard out the back.'

John assured him that the car was the least of the worries. 'The first thing we've got to do is find you a good barrister.' One who could keep the angry Hohola family at bay while John arranged compensation monies.

'But you mustn't pay money,' Francis tried to insist. 'I will go to gaol and pay that way.'

'And get your leg broken when they let you out? Probably get both legs broken.'

'That's my problem.'

'No. It's my problem. It's my responsibility.'

'Thank you, *poro*. But do me one more favour. It will make me happy. I don't want you to put off your holiday.' Then Francis smiled and added, 'Jill will look after me while you're gone.'

The police took Francis to the remand centre at Bomana. His case would not be coming up for six weeks so John decided he would go south to Sydney, leaving Francis in the hands of the legal firm Bowman, Bowman and Kitupai. The lawyers told John that Francis did not stand a chance, he would go to gaol. John told them to defend him vigorously anyway.

On Christmas Day Jill Warwarup drove John to the airport for the morning flight.

They stood under the whirring ceiling fans in the crowded terminal waiting for the boarding call. With difficulty Jill lit a cigarette, shielding it from the fanned air currents. In the noise and confusion John barely heard what she was saying:

'He's such a talented man. And he carries such a load of pressures inside. But it's not his fault. We're the ones who've fucked his life up. And fucked his brain up.' She pushed from her eyes a stray length of blonde hair waving in the air currents.

'I think he spends a lot of his time dreaming about being a kid in his village. Before he went to school. That's his Golden Age,' John suggested.

'And we've given him Progress. Cars to smash into kids with. We've robbed him of his village, haven't we? I feel terrible about it.'

'It's not your fault.'

'It bloody well is.'

She dropped the partly smoked cigarette to the floor and crushed it under the toe of her sandal, then lifted her face in challenge.

The loudspeakers crackled. Jill surprised him by kissing him on the cheek as he turned and headed for the boarding gate.

It was an explosion in slow motion. From Sydney airport he caught a taxi straight to some friends at Potts Point who had a marvellous unit overlooking the harbour. They were entertaining an American boy when he arrived. They welcomed John extravagantly, showered him with kisses at the door. They put their arms around him and pulled him into the apartment. The Christmas tree lights were flashing, the spa was churning, the gourmet fantasies from the rude food shop jutted on trays. His friends poured chardonnay into his tall-stemmed glass, they drew out several lines of cocaine to share. In the huge mirrored bathroom he saw himself and two others reflected endlessly in all directions coupling, coupling, and he, at the centre of a group animal with the Californian boy ball-deep inside him, cried out loud in his ecstasy, 'God, this is civilisation!'

THIRTY-ONE

John began the climb back up the track. He went slowly, trying to conserve his strength. As he went he looked for the Vietnam veteran's shoeprints in sandy patches here and there but could not discern them. He half-wished he had asked the man to help him. *Like Damien Parer's Kokoda Trail soldier.* But he thought better of it, imagining the full consequences.

'*Jesus, what's the matter with you, mate?*'

'*I'm dying of AIDS.*'

'*Oh, Christ, no. A poofter!*'

He toiled on. The bush blurred and spun around him, sharp cold air exploded in his lungs. He stopped at regular intervals to rest, and to listen above the rasp of his breathing for others on the track. He did not want anyone to appear around a bend and take him by surprise. An innocent family, for example.

'*Hullo. Nice day. Are you all right?*'

'*No, actually. I'm dying of AIDS.*'

'*Damien! Kylie! Come this way!*'

He understood the attitude, had been prone to it himself. Was still prone, in a way. There was yet a part of him which felt uncontaminated by his illness, and which resented the fact that it could not walk away, leaving another to suffer.

He sat on a rock beside the track and let the bitter sweat ooze into his greatcoat. With pain at his own memories, he recalled the day he went out to the university library at Kensington. It was five months ago, but that time had no meaning, no length, any more. It was the same day he went for the results of the tests in Surry Hills. They counselled him at the clinic, gave him pamphlets, and suggested he read further books. He left the clinic and caught the bus to the university. He knew his way around the library there, knew the catalogue and the stairways and the floors where different sections were. A computer catalogue had been installed since his undergraduate days, but otherwise things were much the same. On the third floor he found a shelf of books on AIDS, multiple copies mainly, four or five copies each of just half a dozen texts. He did not feel like sitting among the students to read them. He took the books into the men's toilet, remembered his old cubicle, and sat in it for privacy.

He did not know why it had been his favourite cubicle. Perhaps the graffiti was better there? He remembered the textacolor arrow pointing to the toilet paper dispenser and the caption: TOWN PLANNING DEGREES. PLEASE TAKE ONE. He hadn't written it, but wished he had. It had gone now, painted over many times. A new edition of graffiti for each new era, like the Hydro refurbishings. The contemporary scrawl was all about Jesus and safe sex. God, once upon a time graffiti used to be funny.

He read the books. As much as he needed. The pages shook in his hands. How frightening to be totally ignorant of what was happening to your own body. As if your body was a stranger who had gone out and done something you would never do— had had an affair behind your back, you being the last to know. But that was not the major betrayal he felt. What scared him most as he read was the discovery that his mind became the stranger. His body and he were at one, albeit fearfully, researching their problem (their death, basically) but his mind lagged, did not want to read about it, resented the imposition. *You feel all right, don't you? You don't feel you are dying. Not yet you don't.* He found in his head the absurd thought that he might *catch* the disease from the well-thumbed texts in his hands. Wouldn't everyone who imagined they had or did in fact have AIDS come and take these books out, handle them, contaminate them? He forced himself to turn the pages over. He gripped the soft covers, clung to them, knowing that if he could not acknowledge even this much about having the disease then he was doomed to a bad death, a death before death. On the wall beside him someone had written: AIDS—GOD'S GIFT TO GAYS. It was that scrawl which gave him the anger and the strength to continue.

He read fast and furiously. It was study for the biggest examination of his life. He spent the entire afternoon in the cubicle. And, as he knew was the case with all education, the more he learnt the more he knew he needed to know. He grew increasingly dissatisfied. How pointless, he realised, that he should read about Moritz John Kaposi (born Moriz Kohn, 1837–1902) whose sarcoma would soon fill his guts, or that he should swot up on the effects of polymorphonuclear cells and macrophages, when he had never researched Ina Stocks whose genes and madness had run in his blood for decades. To prove the point he quizzed himself: How much of his life was born out of her life, or was woven back into her life? How much of her story, her mind's burden, did he carry in his mind? He sat in the cubicle and recalled the day when she came to the poolside and drew him from the water and led him to her room.

He did not need to look up a single book. He *was* the book.

He came out of the cubicle so grimly determined that he forgot he still clutched the books in his hands until he went through the electronic detector system. There was a shrill *weep-weep-weep* and the barrier locked against his middle. Everyone on the library ground floor turned. A librarian came around from behind the desk saying, 'Don't worry about it. It often goes off like that.'

Through a red hot blush (surely he hadn't blushed since childhood!) he had to explain that he had forgotten he held the books. 'I'm not even a student here,' he apologised.

The woman took the books from him. She could not help but see the titles on their covers. The four-letter acronym. She dropped them gingerly onto the Shelves Return trolley. 'That's all right,' she said, glancing away. She de-activated the barrier. Still not daring to look at him she urged, 'You can go through now'.

From his resting place on the side of the mountain John started up again. There was pain in his guts now. He lugged the weight of the pain, step by step, up the ochre track in the dead silent, khaki bush. He wished for an end to the agony, to solitude, to climbing. Then he began really to worry, because it seemed a possibility that he would not make it.

He moved ahead and looked back at himself toiling, stooped, dead-tired, panting on the track. He marvelled at how old the figure of himself appeared. 'There was a crooked man, who walked a crooked mile...' He stood on the track and waited, and gradually the figure caught up to him. Then he moved ahead.

The bush fell away at the sides of the track and once more the wind blew. He stopped to let it tear at his face and hair. He wiped the scum from his lips and the cold wind tears from his eyes. He pressed ahead and felt the shadow of the hotel come down over him where the track widened and almost lost itself in gutters, and he stumbled and went on all fours the last few metres into the embrace of the rock overhang, the womb of the rock-wave which swelled beneath the cliff top and the Hydro's foundations.

He lay there, up on one elbow in a wind-swirled cleft. The sandstone arched around him, forming a grotto. He leant back against the curved rock face and felt the wind buffet against his form, shuddering in angry eddies in the cave, beginning the slow carving of his shape to a wind-form.

In a panic he scrabbled with his hands on the ground and found a piece of concrete, vaguely flint-shaped. With it he began to scratch on the wall of the cave. He had never done this before in his life. Not on a bus seat, or a school desk, or a lavatory wall. He scraped the soft sandstone away while the wind cleaned off the excess. 'JF WAS HERE,' he wrote. He gouged the letters deeper and deeper, knowing the wind's work would win them, but not for a long time. Then he added the date.

With startling clarity John observed to himself—and for a moment wished that he could share the thought—that it is not simply in these sorts of moments that one's life begins to pass before one's eyes. It is, more significantly, that one's life is given connections and clarities, and cohesion. The point of it all is seen, and, tragically, that point is an abyss. The triteness of it seems appalling. But when you have killed a man—the one you love—everything is appalling.

John lay back and heard his heart belting away inside him. It was something.

THIRTY-TWO

Could he say he had felt her in him at an early age? In his blood as he grew? In his loneliness and his sense of rejection? In his urges to run away? Certainly she was there, invisible, in the nervy household where he grew up. Its labyrinth of fears and guilts and secrecies was due to her. Those locked doors he came up against were locked against her.

'Why doesn't Ina come here to visit us? Why do we always visit her?'

His parents would answer, 'Don't you like going to the Hydro, Johnno?'

'Yes. But she never comes here. I don't know why.'

He would hear them arguing behind the kitchen door:

'Put her in a home.'

'I can't abandon her.'

'It wouldn't be abandoning her.'

'I can't do it.'

He admired his father who was talented, ambitious and hollow-eyed with the pressures of building up his business. But a door kept closing between them.

'He looks like his grandmother.'

'Don't say that, Les. For God's sake.'

His mother clung, desperately in love. He always saw her arm burrowing at the crook of his father's elbow. She would never leave her husband as Ina had done.

Johnno felt he grew up in the hallways of the house at Seaforth. That was his territory—the polished floors, the closed doors.

He looked for Ina.

At three years old he pushed past a broken paling in the back fence and escaped down the kerbless road, through the sandstone cutting, down the bush track and the sandstone steps to the grey boatshed and the jetty. His mother caught up with him at the end of the jetty above the shark-infested waters of Middle Harbour.

'When are we going to see Ina?'

She carried him home kicking, and his father smacked him for it.

'Don't hurt him, Les.'

In the small tubular steel factory Leslie established after the war, he made furniture for sports clubs. When Johnno was five he named a range of club chairs after him. They were sturdy, functional stackers. The 'JF' range.

'Are you going to name a chair after Ina?'

'Forget it, son.'

Johnno eventually learnt to ask the questions that did not disturb his father: the names of stars, of rock forms, of chemicals; how planes flew, how the handbrakes on cars worked.

He locked Ina up inside himself.

'Are we going to the Hydro again these holidays?'

In his own secret language, as in the secret language of the family, the 'Hydro' meant 'Ina'.

And 'golf' meant Ina. And 'Papua' meant Ina. And 'deserted husbands' and 'abandoned children' meant Ina. And after Ina told him her story, 'hanging' and 'black men' and 'sex' and a whole lexicon of unmentionable words meant Ina, Ina, Ina.

It was during his fourteenth summer, the day of his parents' wedding anniversary. They had gone for a walk down one of the gorge tracks. They must have thought he was busy in the Hydro swimming pool, splashing about with the other boys. He came up from under water at one side of the pool and saw Ina above him, her stocky form on the crazy-paved surround, looking down. He had never associated her with the swimming pool. Normally she was indoors, or occasionally on a picnic rug. She stood like a new concrete statue, with the blue water splashing towards her, some of it wetting her long dress, and she gestured with her hand for him to climb out.

In her room he sat dripping wet, shivering, as she placed herself in front of the window and began to speak:

'Your parents only know the story in the newspapers, Johnno. Little Tom was nasty enough to send the cuttings to them after they were married. But I want to tell you the truth, and to do that I must start at the beginning...'

Her story enveloped and entered him. He remembered names he had no faces for and places he had not seen, and words he had no context for understanding. They burrowed into him, along with the lavender smell of her, the disturbing rustle of her skirts over her stockinged thighs, and the nervousness of her hands in her lap. With the story of her dark life and with the tears he saw in her eyes there entered into him a great love for her and her loves, and a great fear of the things she feared. Then she fell apart. The tear tracks broke her face into fragments, her body shuddered with the cumulative horror of her disburdening. As her tower collapsed in front of him he sat as if paralysed. He had no knowledge of how to help her, and no outlet for his distress. He felt her story penetrate him, wind him up, charge him. A long fuse in him started burning. And if he did not understand the links and consequences in what she told him, he knew for certain that she had started a madness and that he must always have that madness whirring in him.

It was dusk in the room when she told him to come to her and she parted her knees so that she could hug him fiercely and long, and then she told him to go.

He sidled along the corridors back to his parents' room. They had not returned, so he sat on his bed without switching the light on, feeling how his swimmers were still damp. He supposed he masturbated then because the story had disturbed him. But the guilt of it was swallowed up in the shock he received when a pearl oozed in the dimness at the end of his penis. It was his first semen.

With confusion whirring in his head, he ran outside to the

floodlit pool and dived in. He swam and swam until his arms and legs ached and his heart was a burning oppression in his chest. Then his parents found him.

'Have you been swimming all this time?' his father asked.

'Yes,' Johnno replied, climbing out of the pool.

A policeman took Ina into custody on the cliff top beyond the tennis courts the next day. She had a seven-iron in her hands and was addressing a ball which lay within a metre of the howling precipice. To get to that lie she had blown big divots out of the lobby carpet and the croquet green. The police informed his parents that she had been taken to the psychiatric hospital near Orange. His mother broke down at the Hydro's reception desk, with the chaos caused by Ina's golfing through the corridors still erupting around her.

Ina lasted only weeks in Bloomfield hospital. She died by hanging herself in the women's toilet. It was a terrible business, and Johnno's mother took it badly. She responded as if Ina had once again betrayed her, her anxiety focused on how Ina had abandoned family decency even further. She passed little of the news on to her son. She seemed to think it was a burden she should bear alone.

Possibly to cast Ina low in Johnno's eyes, his father related his version of the last facts of Ina's life—the golfing down the corridors, the hanging in the hospital—embellished with phrases such as 'round the bend' and 'lost her marbles'. Johnno said with simple insight, 'I know why she's mad.'

His father said no more about it after that, and Johnno thought his father looked at him—perhaps suspicious of Ina's genes.

Johnno was sure Ina's madness put a lid on his father's hopes for him. Johnno was a flawed design, unlike the 'JF' range of club chair which sold in thousands and supported the arses of countless RSL members, football clubbies, golf fanatics, bowls players, and God-knows-what-other-brands of drunken club-goers. But the 'JF' range was entirely his father's creation; there was no contamination from his mother's side of the family.

Some months after Ina's death the Freemans held a Sunday barbecue at the Seaforth house. A 'backyard-warming party' his parents called it. They had bought the vacant lot behind the house and had extended the backyard, landscaped it all the way down to the road below. There was a sandstone flagged barbecue pit and a wide curved set of stairs leading downwards to their own bushland wilderness.

'We've got more than half an acre now,' his father boasted as he poured drinks, the genial host.

The paved area was swarming with Freeman Tubular Products' designs: outdoor chairs, wheeled tables, pot-plant stands. His father had his newest design—a fold-up golf-buggy incorporating a seat—on display. A lot of people arrived. Neighbourhood friends, his father's business friends. They sat in the Freeman Tubular Products chairs, they hung about under the discontinued Freeman Hoist with its patent canvas cover which turned it into a small marquee. The men drank Resch's Pilsener and DA beer in glasses. The women settled for Porphyry Pearl. There were canapes and fancy dips with biscuits, and steak and sausage sandwiches cooked on the new gas 'Waltzing Matilda' barbecue. Everyone talked about the recent Graeme Thorne kidnapping. The weekend papers showed pictures of tracker dogs in use at the Wakehurst Parkway monument where the boy's school bag was found. The only other news to force its way onto the front page of the *Sun-Herald* that morning had been Kel Nagle's win in the British Open.

The barbecue was a great success. Warm Sydney winter weather. The smell of the bush mingled with the smell of outdoor cooking. The voices of kookaburras rose from the bayside below. Smoke drifting, steaks and bangers sizzling. And a bizarre excitement to it all: the £15 000 reward, the suitcase behind the monument just up the road, the possibility that the kidnapper lived close by...was maybe even at the party...No. Couldn't be. A sick suburban joke. The sun sank over Castlecrag and shot the sky with pink. The hired coloured lights which his father had rigged up in the trees and across the patio lit up. The friends drank on, then began leaving. The plastic plates littered the new flagging. The Freeman Tubular Products chairs were left askew. The grease congealed on the barbecue. A breeze blew up from the bay, rattling the eucalypts. With the last guest gone, his father drained a final glass of beer in the clear night, and looked up at the stars. His mother bent over the barbecue, cleaning it with a Wettex.

Then, seated on the wide, curved step of the new flagging, Johnno said, 'Ina told me about Vaimuru before she died.'

Seeing the aghast look on his parents' faces, he added, 'We'll never forget her, will we.'

Thirty-three

Francis spent six months in the Bomana gaol. During that time John arranged the compensation payment for the Hohola people. It was an expensive broken leg. The girl's group tripled their claim when they heard that a white man was paying it, which made Francis furious.

'Don't pay,' he said. 'It's the twentieth century, isn't it? I'll do my payback in gaol.'

Francis had no money in any case, and John preferred the depletion in his own savings to the thought that Francis could be hunted on his release. By paying the compensation he thought Francis would be fairly safe. The one thing in Francis' favour was that the Hohola group knew he was drunk on the night of the accident. At least he had some excuse.

John visited Francis each weekend. He drove out to Bomana in the dust and in the rain. Most weekends Jill accompanied him, but she let him go alone now and then—on purpose, he supposed, so that Francis could be entirely his.

They met in a bare compound along with a hundred other prisoners and visitors. They shook hands and found themselves a space where they could talk, up against the cyclone wire fence.

'What have you brought me, *poro?*'

'A sponge cake. Watch out for the wire cutters inside.'

Francis opened the bag. It was full of betelnut, as usual.

'Thank you, *poro.*'

'How have you been?'

'All right. Things don't change much. A Chimbu was beaten this week.'

'By a warder?'

'Yes. Another Chimbu. Village life goes on here.'

They leant against the wire. Beside them two highlanders held hands unselfconsciously, participating in the traditional custom of male friendship.

'Jill sends her love.'

'Thank you, *poro.*'

'Do you miss her?'

'Yes. And you.'

John smiled. 'Bullshit artist.'

'Why bullshit? I need both of you. That's my Independence. I wish we were having parties. Don't you?'

'Yes. I wish we were.'

'When I get out, we'll have a big party. Okay? Just you and me. We'll have an orgy. Like your Sydney orgies.'

'Not like my Sydney orgies.'

'Better than your Sydney orgies. We'll go crazy.'

They held hands secretly against the wire. The talk smouldered on in fifty languages across the compound. Someone in the crowd laughed. At the touch of Francis' skin John felt the blood marshalling in his groin and at the same time he felt the futility of it.

'One of us has the wrong colour skin, mate.'

'Perhaps both of us have the wrong colour skin, *poro.*'

Francis' hand tightened its grip. John felt the sleek bones inside the smooth, dry fingers.

'I love you, *poro,*' John whispered.

'Time's up,' the warders shouted.

On the weekend of Francis' release they drove out of town along the red dirt road to Bootless Inlet. They had the windows open, wanting the early morning air to rush at them and pummel them with fragrances. They turned down a hot bumpy track they knew well, wound through car-high savannah grass and screw-palms, and came out at last at the isolated beach which looked across a reef-strewn bay to crouching, sun-struck islands.

They tumbled out of the car, out of their clothes. Out of their minds with delight and passion they ran on the smooth dark sand. Drunk with freedom, they hit the water and plunged, grappled, sank, turned each other over, wallowed with the water whelming round them, chest-to-chest, clasped and crushed each other, desperate for the depths within to weld. Then on the hot sand, kiss-crazed, laved in saliva and suntan lotion, love-whipped, they rode each other, reckless cowboys, bolted and bucked, till the skin broke and their bloods exchanged curses beyond their knowing.

The next week, worried about diarrhoea which he thought might he amoebic dysentery, John saw a doctor in Boroko. He was a wise young medic, as it turned out, for although John's was the first case he had seen, the first of its kind in the country, he suggested he go South for tests.

He said goodbye to no one. He stayed late after work then walked across to the executive building where he slipped his letter of resignation under the locked door to the Minister's office. He drove home and parked his car in the garage, leaving the keys in the ignition. Then he went into the house and packed his suitcase. The music cassettes, the novelty bow tie . . . those were memories enough. He could think of nothing more he needed so he closed the case. He sat in the lounge room without the lights on and opened a new bottle of Glenfiddich. He drank straight from the bottle, and waited for the taxi.

On the way to the airport he asked the driver, 'Is this Taxi Number 33?'

The driver's head turned around, grinning. '*Nogat, masta. Em i namba twandi-paib tasol.*'

The driver thought it was a great joke.

THIRTY-FOUR

John crawled up the steps by the tennis courts then stood and walked slowly around to the lobby entrance. He went unsteadily through the lounge and began climbing the stairs to the New Wing. He took the first flight as quickly as he could (though that was painful and slow enough) to escape the stares of a shocked family sitting in the lounge. At the landing, beyond their view, he stopped and waited for the vertigo to leave him, and tried to shift the burden of Francis, now a pain heavier than the threat of dying. One by one he lifted his failing feet, but had to stop another time, slumped against the handrail half way to the top landing. From there he looked upwards at the eternity of stairs and doubted that he could go any further.

He asked the taxi driver to keep driving.

To the west, *poro*. We go to the west, that's where we go. We wander there, just wander till we find the land of the dead. In the land of the dead we sit down and we're happy. We're always happy to look back and see how life goes on. Life goes on and on and pretty soon everyone comes to join us. Everyone wanders west in the end, *poro*.

The driver has put on one of the cassettes. A siren wailing. *Liu liu liu.*

Just keep driving west, *poro*.

One last hole to play. And what a hole it is! Tee on the cliff edge. Blind green. Can't see the flag. You just hit right out there into the sky. Aim at blue. Hope for the best. You drive with love, Johnno. Not with science. Relax now. Arms are very tight. Probably won't have much rhythm. But here we go. Feet planted nicely. Don't address the ball, let it address you. Arms loose, please. Drain the mind of thoughts. A deep breath. Eye on the ball. Then backswing. Hold it. Easy balance. Hips swivelling. Okay, let it swing. Feel gravity. Bring it down. Don't lift the head now. Don't lift the head.

PWANGGGGGG!

TOM FLOOD
Oceana Fine

1988 *Australian*/Vogel winner.
1990 Miles Franklin Award winner.

A tantalising first novel dealing with multiplicity of perception—through history and memory, national mythologies, families and writing (blood and ink) puzzles and their reasons—which might be said to be their execution.

'From realism to surrealism, this is a novel always original, exciting, different.' **Geoffrey Dutton**

'An extraordinarily passionate book.' **Brian Matthews**

'An astonishing first novel.' **A. P. Reimer**